Best wishes,

[signature: Plato Papajohn]

Vicious Mind

a novel by Plato Papajohn

BOOK PUBLISHERS NETWORK

Book Publishers Network
P.O. Box 2256
Bothell, WA 98041
425-483-3040

10 9 8 7 6 5 4 3 2

Printed in the United States of America

LCCN 2004113123
ISBN 0-9755407-8-5

Cover Design: Laura Zugzda
Editor: Vicki McCown
Interior Layout: Stephanie Martindale

To Antoinette,
My Wife and My Best Friend,
The Light of My Life

Contents

Acknowledgement

A huge debt of gratitude is owed to Niki Sepsas and Irene Lafakis of Birmingham, Alabama, and Vicki McCown, Anacortes, Washington for their assistance in making this book a reality. Their efforts will be forever appreciated.

June 4, 2002

The barking of his black Labrador from the side yard alerted Peter Wilson to the mailman's arrival. The excited eight-year-old ran through his home and burst out the front door, just in time to see the mailman walking away to the next house.

"See you tomorrow," the mailman called, waving to the boy.

"Bye," Peter said as he raced to the mailbox. Eagerly removing the mail he found there, the boy ran back into the house and straight to the study. He knew his father would be waiting for him, ready to begin their daily ritual of opening the mail.

"Hey, slow down!" Mike Wilson laughed. "What's your hurry?"

"Dad, I got the mail," Peter said. "Can I open it?"

His father smiled at the boy fondly. "Sure. Bring it over here."

Mike Wilson reached into the top center drawer of his polished oak desk and brought out a letter opener, which he handed to Peter.

"Here, you can use this, but it's sharp so—"

"I know, I know," interrupted Peter, "be careful not to cut myself."

Solemnly, Peter picked up the ornate letter opener. For the hundredth time he admired how the decorated handle felt smooth to the touch, how the nine-inch blade glistened in the sunlight. Then, turning to the pile of mail, he slowly opened and removed the contents of each letter.

When he finished, he handed the pile to his father. In doing so, the opener slipped out of Peter's hand and fell to the floor. He quickly glanced up at his dad, his face creased by a worried brow.

"Sorry, Dad," he apologized. Then seeing his dad's forgiving smile, he bent to retrieve the opener. Straightening up, Peter grinned impishly and waved the opener almost threateningly at his father. "I've got you now, Dad. Hands up!"

Mike Wilson laughed and raised his hands over his head.

"You've got me, all right," he conceded. "What are you going to do? Kill me?"

"Oh, no, Dad," Peter replied. "I'd never hurt you."

"Well, thank goodness for that," said Mike.

Peter sat down in a chair across from his father, his attention once again captured by the unique letter opener. As Mike Wilson gazed at the sleek blade in the boy's hands, his mind wandered back to a day when he had been hardly older than Peter—a day that would be forever seared in his memory.

On that sunny, summer morning Mike Wilson had peered from behind the kitchen door to see his enraged father, Bill, with both hands encircling his wife's throat. Momentarily motionless, Mike watched the terror wash over his mother's face as his giant-like father slowly strangled the life out of her. Then, without thinking, Mike burst through the door.

"Dad! Stop it! Dad!" he screamed. "You're killing Mom! Stop! Stop it!"

Mike's father never took his eyes off his wife's face despite his son's entreaties. His face turned a fiery crimson, and the muscles in his strong arms remained taut as his large hands maintained their death grip on his wife's throat. Mike's mother opened her mouth, but no sound escaped as she turned her bruised and blackened eyes on the man who was trying to kill her.

The young boy ran toward his father. In vain, he tried to pull the giant away from his mother. Finally, Bill Wilson eased his right hand from his wife's throat. With the sweep of his huge arm, much like the motion of an annoyed bear, he shoved the boy away. Landing in a heap in a corner of the kitchen, Mike looked desperately around the room. His mind raced, frantically trying to figure out what he should do. Then it came to him. He ran to the kitchen counter, opened the top right-hand drawer, and extracted a large carving knife. Turning back to his parents, he saw them still locked in a death struggle on the floor. For a second, he hesitated, standing there trembling. Tears streamed down his face, yet he knew what he had to do. Gathering all his strength, he brought the knife down, plunging it into the right side of his father's back, a blow that, as he would learn later, pierced a kidney.

Mike Wilson, still on his mental journey, heard a distant voice—his young son speaking to him in the here and now.

"Dad, *Dad*," he heard Peter's voice say insistently. "Aren't you going to look at all the letters I've opened?"

Mike, realizing where he was, felt a chill go down his spine.

"Peter, come here and sit on my lap," he said. A soft smile washed over his face as he watched his son come to him.

With a neat jumping twist, Peter landed on his father's lap. "Did I open the mail okay?" he asked, doubt clouding his clear blue eyes.

"Yes, you did, thanks," Mike said. "You know I love you very much, don't you?"

"Sure, Dad," the boy replied. "I love you very much, too!"

Mike Wilson kissed the boy's forehead and squeezed him tightly.

"Well," Mike said, "you know we have big plans for your birthday today, right?"

The boy beamed and nodded excitedly.

"Tell me again," he said. "Tell me what's going to happen today."

"Well, I have a feeling there'll be a good-sized birthday party this after-noon. For one thing, all your friends will be here. Plus, it looks like your grandmother is coming. I bet she has a very special surprise for you, too."

"What do you think it is?" Peter asked excitedly. "Do you know?"

"Sorry, I can't tell; you'll just have to wait and see. She should be here pretty soon."

Just then, the telephone rang. Mike reached around his son to answer it. "Hello?"

"May I speak with Mike Wilson?" a voice on the other end asked.

"This is he," Mike replied.

"Mr. Wilson," the voice began, "my name is Tim Stewart. I'm the war-den at the Louisiana State Correctional Facility in Evangeline Parish."

"Hold on a second, please," Mike said. Putting down the receiver, he turned to Peter. "Son, I have some business here on the phone. Why don't you go and see if you can help your mom get ready for the birthday party?"

"Okay, Dad," the boy said.

Mike eased Peter off his lap and watched the boy as he scampered out of the room. He then turned back to the telephone.

"I'm sorry, Mr. Stewart," Mike Wilson said. "Please continue."

"Mr. Wilson, it is my duty as correctional facility warden to notify the next of kin of the death or impending death of any of our inmates. Your father, Bill Wilson, is dying of cancer. The correctional facility doctors feel he has very little time left. He requested the services of a Catholic priest to hear his confession. This is a common practice among many incarcerated individuals who are facing death, either by execution or from natural causes, and a priest has visited him. Your father also asked us to contact you as his son and next of kin. He asked me to tell you that he would like to see you before he dies."

Mike Wilson remained silent for a moment. The warden's message had opened a floodgate of memories.

"Thank you for phoning me, Mr. Stewart," he said. "I'll let you know if I decide to visit him."

He hung up the phone, but did not move, simply staring at it for a while. His mind turned again to another day of long ago.

The genealogy of the Wilson clan has always been a bit fuzzy. Most likely they originally came to the new country from England, but the "when" and "why" were never recorded. History first takes note of the Wilsons in the early 1800s, when two brothers, John and James, showed up in Louisiana. With no apparent skills but plenty of cunning, they became successful in the early days of the country's expansion, earning a certain prosperity through a variety of shady and sometimes illegal ventures.

Their modern-day saga began with Mike Wilson's grandfather, Eric. Because Eric's father, Thomas, had added to the family fortune through a series of shrewd, if somewhat questionable, land dealings in Louisiana in the late nineteenth century, Eric was born into what was considered an old-money Louisiana family in 1902 in the town of Plaquemine, not far from Baton Rouge. Eric became the heir-apparent to the family's vast commercial and agricultural enterprises, the glittering centerpiece of which was Oakleigh, a sprawling complex featuring a cotton plantation, ginning operation, and shipping center just south of Baton Rouge located near Plaquemine on the Mississippi River.

By the time he turned thirty years old, Eric had seen both parents pass on to whatever rewards or punishments they were to receive in the next life. They left their son at the helm of the empire, a job for which Eric proved to be well suited. As generous as he was charming, his contributions to various organizations had made him one of the most loved and respected men in the state.

In 1934, he had married the former Debra Moxley, a demure Mississippi belle, with a family tree almost as old and stately as the Wilsons'. With Debra at his side, Eric went on to expand the dynasty, posting impressive successes in diversifying the family's business dealings and expanding into foreign markets. The couple had two children: a daughter, Kristi, in 1935 and a son, Bill, two years later.

Kristi was the quintessential golden child who relished the princess role into which she had been born. Gilt-framed portraits that glorified the auburn-haired beauty with dark flashing eyes hung in prominent places throughout Oakleigh's thirty rooms of opulence. Following a perfect childhood, Kristi attended an old Southern college where she earned a bachelor's degree in economics and graduated with many honors. Shortly after her season as a debutante, she married a successful stockbroker, Mr. Steve Walker. They enjoyed a wonderful marriage and frequently visited Oakleigh to attend the lavish parties held there. Soon the marriage was blessed with two children, twins Misty and Jeff. Kristi, with all of her accomplishments, became the pride and satisfaction of her parents.

From his earliest years, Kristi's younger brother, Bill, portrayed the other side of the family coin. Intimidated by his older sister and envious of the attention lavished on her by his parents, Bill developed a rebellious spirit. As a restless teen with an uncontrollable temper, Bill often found himself in hot water at school and with the local police. The family name and extensive influence had, on more than one occasion, extricated the hot-tempered youngster from incidents that grew increasingly serious.

Bill became the epitome of the spoiled, rich kid. He wore expensive clothes and drove a variety of imported sports cars. "The faster the better" was his motto. His wild and lavish lifestyle more than earned him the nickname "Rich Boy Billy."

As he grew older, he accelerated quickly into the fast lane. His passion for fast cars was surpassed only by his obsession with women. He became a familiar figure in the backroom gambling dens of New Orleans and attracted a lively following of jet setters and bottom feeders. They were eager to help him spend his money, drink his liquor, smoke his pot, and draw out a few lines of his cocaine.

Despite this self-destructive lifestyle, Bill had a way about him that was irresistible. Charming and extremely intelligent, he breezed through his undergraduate program at Tulane. Then, inspired by his father's bribe of a new Ferrari, he went on to complete law school and pass the Louisiana State Bar exam on the first try. But he had no intention of practicing law. Instead, Bill contented himself with maintaining a bloodshot eye on the few segments of the family business with which his father had entrusted him. His one real talent seemed to be his ability to hire and place qualified managers in key positions to keep the daily wheels of business turning smoothly.

As the elder Eric Wilson approached traditional retirement age, he wanted to turn more of the business over to his son, but Bill had yet to display enough initiative and responsibility to prove he could fill his father's shoes. Eventually, however, the opportunity to do so finally came.

The International Cotton Growers Association held its annual conference in Atlanta, Georgia, each spring. While Bill had accompanied his father previously to several of these gatherings, most of his time had been spent at the hotel bar or hitting on women at the numerous hospitality suites sponsored by vendors buttonholing clients at the event. Bill had made many promises in the past to his father that he would change and devote himself to the family business, but those promises always fell through. He still had too many "hobbies" his father tolerated, simply because he wanted to have a relationship with his son. In 1966, however, as Bill approached his twenty-ninth birthday, Eric decided to send Bill alone to the conference to represent Wilson Enterprises. If the younger Wilson had not yet developed enough ability to stand and walk alone by now, he never would.

Arriving to Atlanta's Hartsfield International Airport, Bill took a cab to the downtown Hyatt Hotel where the conference was being held. After checking into his suite, he gravitated to the lobby bar, where he quickly downed a couple of glasses of Dewar's on the rocks. He signed his bill, then sauntered through the hotel's gleaming lobby to check the activities board. As he searched the board for the registration room, he noticed a woman walking toward him, smiling. He stood riveted to the spot as though hit by a thunderbolt.

In her late twenties, Judy Freeman represented the epitome of the female professional. Tall and slender; she wore long blonde hair perfectly coiffed to frame a face with high cheekbones, dazzling blue eyes, a slightly turned-up nose, and teeth that belonged in a toothpaste commercial. Her long, aquiline neck tapered into square shoulders that were further accentuated by a well-cut navy-blue jacket, the top half of an expensive and stylish business suit. With an air of confidence, she walked straight up to Bill.

"How do you do, Mr. Wilson," she said, extending her hand. "My name is Judy Freeman. I'm the conference coordinator for the International Cotton Growers Association."

Stunned, Bill shook the extended hand, noticing the firm handshake she offered.

"It's a pleasure," he said, still off guard.

"I wanted to introduce myself to you," she began. "Although we've never met, I know your father from other association events, and I knew who you were. Is your father also at the conference this year?"

"No," Bill replied. "I'm the only Wilson representing the family this year. I hope you're not disappointed."

"Not at all," she laughed. "I wanted to tell you to feel free to call on me if you need any assistance. I can help you arrange private meetings with other growers or some of the shippers. I'll be happy to help in any way."

"I'll keep that in mind," Bill said with an impish look in his eye. Judy, picking up on the flirtatious look, decided to ignore it.

"Great!" she said, again extending her hand. "I hope to see you around."

"You can count on it," Bill said, flashing his most engaging smile.

He watched her walk across the lobby to join a group of men talking near the elevators. Bill realized then and there what his goal would be for the conference. He had been with a great many beautiful women in his life, and at age thirty-one, he considered himself a confirmed bachelor, the consummate playboy. Watching Judy Freeman interact with other people, however, and noticing the effect she had on them, he suddenly realized that this was a woman with whom he wanted to have more than just a passing fling at a business meeting.

During the next few hours, his interest in Judy Freeman grew overpowering. Throughout the afternoon, he observed her methodically and professionally going about her business. She met with groups and individuals, checked on the status of events planned for the evening, and coordinated the unloading of a late-arriving vendor's exhibit booth. She didn't stop for a break until late in the afternoon, when she walked out the side doors of the hotel to the patio bar near the swimming pool. She took a seat at the bar and waited while the bartender poured a frozen margarita into a salt-rimmed glass for a customer at the other end of the counter.

Bill, who had followed her outside, saw his chance.

"That looks pretty refreshing," he said sliding onto a stool next to her. "May I order one for you?"

Startled, Judy turned, surprised to see Bill.

"Hi," she said and smiled. "You certainly may. I've been going nonstop all afternoon, and I think that's exactly what I need for a pick-me-up. Thanks very much."

"My pleasure," Bill replied. "Excuse me," he called out to the bartender, "one of those for the lady and a Dewar's on the rocks for me."

"I've been watching you," he said to Judy. "You've really had your hands full today. Looks like you work well under pressure."

"Why, thank you, Mr. Wilson," Judy said.

"Please, it's Bill," he said. "The only 'Mr. Wilson' is my father, and like I told you earlier, he's not here. I'm just Bill."

"'Just Bill' it is, then," she smiled.

The bartender placed their drinks in front of them.

"Here's to 'Nice to meet you,' Bill," she said, raising her margarita.

"Nice meeting you, too," he answered, clinking her glass with his. "Judy, may I ask you a question?" he heard himself blurt out. When she nodded her assent, he suddenly found himself tongue-tied. All he could do was stare at her.

She looked at him inquiringly. "You said you had something to ask me. Have you changed your mind?"

"No…its just that…it has absolutely nothing to do with the conference," Bill said. "I'd like to know who you are, where you live, and whether or not you are married."

Chuckling, she ran her finger around the edge of her glass then put the finger to her lips and licked the salt she had collected.

"That's three questions in one. You certainly get to the point, don't you?"

"I like to lay my cards right on the table," Bill said. "Since I met you, I decided that I'd like to get to know you. No sense in playing games. I figure if you'd like to have a drink and talk, fine. If not, you appear to be the type of woman who will tell me so."

"That's fair enough," Judy said. "I'm originally from Denver and have been working as an events coordinator and meeting planner for about four years. I was married once, but it didn't work out. Right now I'm seeing someone back home, but with the way I travel, it seems like we see each other less and less."

"Is it a serious relationship?"

"I'm not sure that's any of your business," she answered, slightly annoyed at his directness.

"I told you that I lay my cards right out," Bill countered. "I'm being honest. You really got my attention, and I'd like to ask you out, but only if you're not involved in a serious relationship."

"And if I answered 'yes,' then you wouldn't ask me out? That seems to strike a noble chord in this day and age."

"Well," he smiled, "maybe I would hesitate a little, but I'm not sure. Like I said, you really turned my head."

"Well, I'm certainly flattered. You know how to give a compliment." Judy lifted the wide-mouthed glass to her lips and took a sip of her marguerita. "How about you? Are you married? I know you and your father have a very successful family business in Louisiana, but that's all I've got on you."

He smiled and took a long swallow of his Scotch. "No," he answered, "I've had women in my life, but I never married or settled down. A lot of people would add 'or grown up' to that list, too."

Judy let out a laugh—a lilting, genuinely warm laugh. "I might have reached that conclusion on my own," she added. They fell silent, each lost in thought.

"Listen," Bill began, "it's about 5:30, and the next business session isn't until seven o'clock. How about a quick something to eat here at the hotel? I promise to have you back in time for work or whatever arrangements you'll need to make before the session starts."

"Actually, that sounds pretty good. I was so busy all day that I missed lunch, and I know I won't have time for anything until later. Let's do it."

"Great," Bill said. "If you like, we can get something quick now and maybe go for dinner somewhere in town after the meeting."

"Let's just see how things go," she said. "We can decide later."

Bill signaled the bartender and paid for the drinks. He and Judy walked through the lobby and up the escalator to the café on the second level. A waiter seated them at a table next to a huge picture window. He took their order for two appetizers and another round of drinks, with Judy joining Bill in ordering a Scotch. Their conversation flowed easily, centering around his home life in Louisiana, her work, and the cotton industry in general.

As they sat chatting, Bill felt the pace beginning to quicken. Was it his imagination or was their eye contact getting longer? Their laughter seemed natural and spontaneous. He sensed that Judy felt as relaxed and comfortable as he did. When they finished their appetizers, she surprised him by asking if he would mind if she smoked.

"Not at all," he said.

"Do you smoke?" she asked.

"Occasionally."

Judy sat back in her chair, appearing much more at ease than he expected her to be after such a brief encounter. He decided to take the lead.

"Judy," he began, "I find you to be an intelligent, beautiful, and very sexually appealing woman. As I said earlier, I've known a lot of women, and I've had a lot of relationships, most of which were very casual. You've captivated me, body and soul. Just these last couple of hours around you has convinced me that I want to know you and see more of you."

Judy took a long draw on her Marlboro and looked deep into his eyes. He felt she could see all the way into his soul.

"You don't seem to have a shortage of lines, do you?"

"It may sound that way, but I assure you that I'm being honest. I'm too old to play games."

"So now I'm supposed to believe that I'm this unbelievably special woman you've been waiting to meet and we waltz off to your bed?"

"Judy," he replied, "I don't know what's going to happen tomorrow, and right now I don't care. All I know is that I am shell-shocked over you."

Again her gaze remained on him, deep and penetrating.

"I could almost believe you," she said. "Either you're pretty well rehearsed with all this or you're telling the truth. I have a feeling it's the former, but if it's the latter, then I am very flattered."

"In that case, tell me you'll have dinner with me after the session ends. I know some very good restaurants in Atlanta, a couple just a short cab ride from the hotel. What do you say?"

She took another long drag from her cigarette, then surprised Bill with her next words.

"Why not?" she smiled. "It might be easier to go to one of the restaurants here at the hotel, though, or," she added with a flash in her eyes, "maybe just order room service."

For a man accustomed to being free and easy with pick-up lines, Bill found Judy's response to be a bit of a shock. The look on his face evidently betrayed him.

"Well, sure," he stammered, "whatever's easiest."

Bill signaled the waiter, signed his suite number, and walked Judy back to the lobby.

"Thanks for the drinks and appetizers," she said.

"Thanks for the company," he replied. "I know you'll be busy for the next few hours. Shall we meet here around ten o'clock, after everything winds down?"

"Sounds good," Judy said. She extended her hand, and Bill felt her professional side returning. She was back on the clock. "See you around ten."

Elated, Bill entered the ballroom, which had been set up theater-style for the meeting. A series of speakers addressed the crowd of almost four hundred people, but Bill's mind was light-years away. All he could think about was Judy, the drinks, dinner, conversation, and her comments, which he analyzed over and over for the duration of the two-hour session. Was she playing with him or was she genuinely interested? Was she as adept at manipulating a situation as he was? Had he met his match in the mating ritual arena? He glanced at his watch repeatedly, eager for the interminable meeting to end.

Finally, around 9:45, the final speaker announced the close of the session and their adjournment until nine the next morning. Bill was among the first to leave the room.

He leaned against one of the portable bars set up for delegates outside the ballroom and ordered a Dewar's. His eyes scanned the lobby for signs of Judy.

He finally sighted her leaving the ballroom and entering the lobby with two men. She was taking notes as they spoke simultaneously to her. Then she smiled and shook her head repeatedly. Bill guessed the men were inviting her for drinks or dinner, but Judy simply shook hands with them and then walked over to where he was standing.

"Looks like someone else is as interested in spending time with you as I am," he said as she approached.

Judy smiled.

"Do I detect a hint of jealousy?" she asked.

"More than a hint. I've been counting the minutes at that meeting, waiting to see you. I thought it would never end."

"Again with the clever lines? You do know what to say to make a woman feel good."

"I'm sure that I am not the first man to compliment you. Are we still on for dinner?"

"Sure, but I'll be honest with you. I'd rather get something here at the hotel than go out. It's been a long day, and my feet are killing me."

"Well, the Brasserie upstairs is very good, but if you're serious about ordering room service, the view from my suite is much better. There's a living room, a small dining room, and if your feet are really tired, you can take your shoes off."

Bill felt his face flush after extending the offer. Social sparring had always come easy to him, but here was Judy Freeman suddenly reducing him to a rank amateur.

"Let's go for the view, then," she said with a coy smile. "But first I'd like a drink." She turned to the bartender. "May I have an Absolut martini, please, with two olives?"

"And another Dewar's here," Bill added.

Most of the delegates were leaving the lobby, and the few who remained sat clustered around in small, scattered groups. Soon Bill and Judy were the only ones left at the bar.

"Would you like to take the drinks upstairs?" Bill asked.

"Let's finish these here and let the crowd thin out before we get on the elevator together," Judy suggested. "Plenty of opportunity for rumors at these events."

"Fine with me," Bill agreed, elated that his plans were moving even quicker than he dared hope.

When they finished their drinks they walked to the elevator, which they rode in silence as it made its ascent. Finally it stopped at the twenty-fifth floor. As they exited, Bill reached into his pocket for the room key and opened the door to his penthouse suite.

Night of June 5, 1966

Judy let out a little gasp as they entered the luxurious suite, astonishment written across her face. Bill grinned at her wide-eyed enthusiasm, then led her through the foyer and into series of split-level rooms. The sprawling living room featured a black leather sofa, arranged with two plush leather chairs around a glass coffee table. A highly polished cherry wood entertainment center occupied an entire wall. Against the opposite wall sat a well-stocked wet bar and mini-kitchen. The intimate dining area, furnished with another glass table and four wrought-iron chairs, cozied up to a picture window that offered a magnificent view of Atlanta. Open double doors revealed a huge bedroom with a king-size bed and private bath.

Judy whistled. "Wow! I'd heard these suites were impressive, but I didn't dream they'd be anything like this. You could put my apartment back home in a corner of this place." She looked over at Bill, a new appreciation reflected in her eyes. "You do travel in style."

Bill walked over to the wet bar while Judy strolled around the living room. "Another martini?" he asked "Or would you rather switch to Scotch?"

"A martini will be fine," she said.

"Two olives, right?"

"You have a good memory."

"Only when it's something I want to remember."

Giving Bill a mock reproving look, Judy moved over to the bar. Sliding onto one of the barstools, she reached into her purse and brought out her cigarettes. Seeing this, Bill picked up a matchbook from the bar's ashtray and struck a match. Leaning over the bar, he lit her cigarette, steadying her hand as he did so. Judy took a long drag, and then exhaled a plume of smoke toward the ceiling.

"Thanks."

Bill finished mixing Judy's martini, then poured a Dewar's for himself. "Here's to good memories," he said, raising his glass.

Judy held her glass aloft, returning his toast, then took a drink. Bill noticed her dainty sips had become healthy swigs.

"Let's order something from room service," Bill suggested. "What are you in the mood for?"

Judy thought for a minute. "Why don't you surprise me? You're doing pretty well so far."

Bill's felt a hot flash of anticipation travel from his chest to his groin. Was it his imagination or had Judy just accelerated the pace of the encounter?

He picked up a room service menu that lay by the phone and dialed the proper extension.

"Room service? This is Suite 2500. I'd like two steaks, medium-rare—" he glanced over at Judy who nodded, "—and the lobster plate. Add a couple of Caesar salads and the best-tasting dessert you've got. Oh, and bring up a bottle of Moët Chandon with that, please…Okay, thanks."

"That sounds great," Judy said. "Actually, I like most anything but fish. I've never developed a taste for it." She swirled the last swallow of gin in her martini glass. "It's a good thing I'm not Catholic."

Bill laughed, then walked over to the sliding glass doors. "Hey, come get a load of this view." As Judy moved to join him, he stood close but made sure he didn't touch her. He wanted to make certain that any overtures came from her. They spent the next several minutes identifying landmarks on the Atlanta skyline and making small talk about the conference.

"Let me freshen that," Bill offered, taking Judy's empty glass. "I need a refill myself."

Judy followed Bill to the bar, leaning on it as he mixed her another martini and refilled his Scotch. Taking her refilled glass, she speared one of her olives. With her eyelids lowered seductively, Judy met Bill's gaze. Slowly, the olive found its way to her lips, where it lingered, then disappeared into her mouth.

There could be no misreading that message, Bill thought

Small talk continued. They had almost finished their drinks when they heard a light knock on the door. Bill opened it, and a polite bellman wheeled in a cart laden with food warmers, a napkin-covered basket of warm bread, and an ice bucket with a magnum of champagne. Bill signed the ticket and gave the bellman a tip as he led him back to the door. Then he turned to Judy.

"Dinner is served."

He placed the meals on the dining room table, put the champagne next to his chair, and pulled Judy's chair back for her. He lifted the plate covers off to reveal steaming entrees of steak and lobster, serving Judy first and then himself.

"Mmmm. That smells divine," cooed Judy.

Bill opened the champagne and poured each of them a glass. As they clinked their glasses, he scanned Judy's face. Her smile and relaxed manner convinced him she felt comfortable—and possibly a bit buzzed from her drinks.

Conversation came easily for both of them as they began a spirited assault on their "surf and turf." Bill appreciated Judy's healthy appetite; she had admitted that the long day's activities had left her famished. She had finished her salad and lobster and eaten most of her filet before placing her napkin on the table. Then she leaned back into her chair and reached for her champagne glass, which Bill had made a point of keeping filled.

"That was absolutely delicious," she sighed.

"Made all the more so by the company," Bill replied smoothly.

"You always know the right thing to say, don't you?"

"I try. Like to go out on the balcony?"

"Let me just make a trip to the ladies' room first."

Bill left the dishes on the table, but took the champagne bucket to the bar where he again filled their glasses. A few minutes later, Judy joined him and lit a cigarette. When she saw Bill give her a look, she blushed.

"I know, I smoke too much, but just after a great meal is one of the best times to enjoy a cigarette," she explained.

"Maybe you'll tell me the other best times," he said.

"Maybe."

Once again, Bill felt a searing thrill shoot through him.

Bill handed Judy her champagne glass. "Come on," he said.

Walking across the room to the sliding glass door, he unhitched the latch and pulled the door open. Judy stepped out onto the balcony, then moved cautiously to the railing where she peered over the side.

"Whew!" she exclaimed "That's frightening even without the champagne. Beautiful view, though, isn't it?"

Bill looked straight at her. The breeze caressed her hair, and the moonlight danced in her eyes.

"Breathtaking," he said.

Judy smiled and turned to look out at Atlanta. Thousands of lights twinkled back at her from far below. Burned by Sheridan during the Civil War, Atlanta had risen like a phoenix from its ashes. Now it was well on its way to becoming a major metropolis with millions of inhabitants.

"Wish we could freeze this frame and hold it for a while," she said.

"For as long as you like," Bill said.

She turned to look at him.

"I wish I could believe you," she whispered.

"Do you want a polygraph?" he asked. "I'll be glad to oblige."

Bill moved closer to Judy; as he did so, she let her eyes close. He placed his index finger on her high cheekbones, then traced the curve of her eyebrows, the length of her nose, and the fullness of her lips. When he finished, she opened her eyes and looked up at him dreamily.

"That's hypnotic," she purred.

"Didn't I tell you I'm a hypnotist?" he asked. He pulled her to him and kissed her lightly on the lips, then leaned back slightly, searching her face for a clue. Judy's eyes were still closed from the kiss, a small smile lingering on her lips. Then, she drew Bill tightly to her. Her lips hungrily sought his as they locked in a fiery embrace that took Bill's breath away. Her hands tussled his hair, while he kissed her cheeks and then slowly ran his tongue down her long, slender neck. He felt her breathing quicken. She kissed him harder and drew him even tighter against her. Bill could feel her body, taut and trembling, intoxicating him. He began unbuttoning her white satin blouse. In response, she tugged at the knot of his tie.

No mistaking where this is headed now, Bill thought. Still, he was a bit stunned at how quickly they had reached this point of no return.

He pulled back slightly from her. She opened her eyes and looked at him inquisitively.

"Something wrong?" she asked.

"Location," he said with an impish grin. "No need to be out here for all Atlanta to watch us when I've already paid for a grand suite inside."

"Let's relocate then," Judy whispered.

Taking her hand, Bill led Judy back inside. At the bar, he pressed his body hard against hers as they locked in another breathless kiss. She swayed softly as she felt his passion rising.

They resumed undressing in earnest, Bill unbuttoning Judy's blouse, she loosening his belt and pulling it free of his pants. Then Judy's frantic hands moved to the buttons on Bill's shirt.

Bill's mind reeled. This gorgeous woman, someone he had just met, appeared to be more aroused than he was, eager to move at an even quicker pace to fulfill his fantasy.

He pulled her blouse free at the same time she loosened his shirt. She began kissing his chest and running her tongue along his neck. He pulled her back.

"Me first," he said. "You just relax."

Judy closed her eyes as Bill began softly kissing the nape of her neck and proceeding down to her breasts. He unclasped her bra and let it fall to the floor, as he ran his tongue lightly over her torso. Judy trembled in ecstasy under his touch.

Bill dropped to his knees and continued kissing her while unbuckling the black leather belt that held her skirt. She wriggled out of the skirt and let it fall to the floor. He kissed her stomach and moved downward. Judy moaned slightly, holding on to the bar for support, as Bill slowly drew her black bikini down and steadied her as she stepped out of it.

Bill stood up and kissed Judy fiercely, a kiss she returned with a passion, her fingernails digging into his back. He stooped down and picked her up in his arms. She was smiling as she looked deeply into his eyes.

"Do I get to bring my drink with me?" she asked.

"I'll come back for it later."

Bill carried Judy into the bedroom and placed her gently on the bed. She immediately sat up, her hand moving to the zipper of Bill's trousers as he stood over her. But in her feverish anticipation, Judy caught the zipper on the material. She looked up at Bill helplessly and they both laughed.

"You take too damn long," he said, a big grin on his face.

Quickly he unstuck the zipper, kicked off his trousers, dropped his briefs, slid off his socks, and jumped into bed. Legs and arms entwined, they locked in an embrace. Bill felt as though he were on fire. The scent of her hair, the feel of her naked body pressed tightly against his, her nails running gently up his back all conspired to drive him into oblivion. For a man accustomed to controlling the situation, he'd never been on a ride quite like this. He felt lucky to be on board.

For the next hour, Bill and Judy hovered on the brink of ecstasy. Then, in an ultimate moment of unbridled passion, they erupted together in convulsive waves of pleasure that seemed to reverberate throughout the room, leaving them quivering and spent.

Finally, they drifted off to sleep in each other's arms.

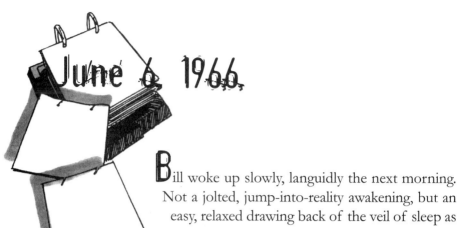

June 6, 1966

Bill woke up slowly, languidly the next morning. Not a jolted, jump-into-reality awakening, but an easy, relaxed drawing back of the veil of sleep as he surfaced into a state of semi-consciousness. His eyes still closed, he rolled over and reached out to Judy's side of the bed.

He found it empty.

His eyes sprang open, and he sat up in bed, glancing quickly around the room. Clearly he was alone. Puzzled, he hopped out of bed and walked first to the bathroom and then into the living room. No one. He noticed that Judy's clothes, which had been strewn about the floor, were gone.

Then something caught his eye—a piece of paper taped to the mirror behind the bar. He crossed the room and snatched it down.

"Thanks for the evening," it read. " Hope to see you at the conference."

Bill tossed the note on the sofa and headed into the bathroom where he hurriedly shaved and raced through a shower. Dressing in his unofficial conference uniform of dark suit, white shirt, and light blue silk tie, he left his room and walked quickly down the hallway to the elevators. As he pressed the "down" button, a glance at his watch told him it was almost 8 A.M.

When the elevator doors opened at the mezzanine level, Bill got off and made his way to the coffee shop. As he waited behind a gaggle of conferees to give his name to the hostess, he spied Judy sitting at a table in the corner. Without hesitation, he brushed by the smiling hostess and walked directly to Judy's table. She looked up, seemingly surprised to see him.

"Good morning, Bill," she said.

"I'm not so sure it is a good morning," Bill replied. "You left without waking me, without saying anything to me. I must have disappointed you last night."

"Quite the contrary," Judy smiled. "Everything was perfect. The suite, the meal, the drinks, and the timing. Now it's time to get back to work, to the real world."

Bill's heart sank. Last night Judy had been so warm, so open, even eager. This morning she seemed distant, an air of casual, nonchalance about her, as though last night had never happened.

"I've got to see you again," Bill said, a note of urgency in his voice.

"Bill, listen to me," she began. "Last night was great, but it also wasn't a very good idea. When the conference wraps up today, you'll go your way, and I'll go mine. You live near Baton Rouge; I live in Denver. That makes dating a little difficult." Judy took a sip of her coffee, cradling the cup in both hands. "Let's leave yesterday where it was, a lovely memory. I'm at a point in my life right now where I need to work a few things out, do some soul searching. I don't want to get involved with anyone at the moment, and it wouldn't be fair to lead you on. I have my reasons, which I don't want to go into right now. But, trust me, it's better this way. Last night…well, last night was just something that, at the time, seemed right—for both of us. I hope you don't think badly of me. You said earlier you believed in being totally honest, and that's what I'm being now with you."

Bill stared at her, momentarily dumbstruck. When words finally came to him, he spoke them slowly, deliberately.

"Judy, I want to, *have* to, see you again," he said. "It's more than what we did last night. You aren't just any woman. I've been nuts about you since I saw you."

"Oh, come on," Judy laughed, "we definitely haven't gone that far in all this. We had a great night. I'm not going to say I didn't enjoy it. But this was just one of those things—a 'business trip encounter.' If we meet again at another conference, you may be just as serious about someone else you meet." She put down the coffee cup and looked at him levelly. "Think about it, Bill. You know I'm right."

"I know I'm crazy about seeing you again."

With a sigh, Judy pushed her plate away and turned to get her purse. Then, sliding out of the booth, she stood up and fixed her striking blue eyes on Bill.

"I'm going to ask you to please respect my feelings," she said. "Let's shake hands and walk away for the time being. Maybe at a later date, things will be different. But right now, I've got some issues to resolve. I hope you understand." She held out her hand and flashed the now familiar smile. "It was truly a pleasure to meet you, Mr. Wilson," she said. "I do hope we meet again."

Bill looked deep into her eyes as he took the outstretched hand.

"You can count on it," he smiled. "Take whatever time you need. I'm a very patient man."

Extracting her hand from Bill's grasp, Judy walked past him. He turned to watch her as she stopped at the cashier's stand to sign her check, then headed to the elevators for the short ride to the first floor conference rooms. She never looked back.

Bill was still standing there, deep in thought, when the waiter came to clear the table.

"Can I get you something, sir?" he asked.

"What...?" Bill answered absent-mindedly, then, startled, he said sheepishly, "No, thank you." Flushed with embarrassment, he strode out of the coffee shop.

He returned to his suite to pack, then checked out at the front desk, asking a bellman to store his bags until his departure later that morning. Straightening his tie, he moved purposefully through the sprawling lobby of the Hyatt to the cavernous ballroom, the room scheduled for the association's closing session.

Because the meeting had already begun, Bill quietly took a seat in the back of the room. Scanning the audience, he spotted Judy in a far corner where she sat demurely, scribbling notes on a pad in her attaché case. Some speaker was droning on about the important work facing the association in the coming year. After sitting through the proceedings for nearly an hour, his mind persistently wandering back to the evening before, Bill decided to leave. He retrieved his luggage from the bell captain and hailed a taxi for the airport. The airline check-in, short flight back to Baton Rouge, and hour's drive home to suburban Oakleigh were all a blur. His mind had no room for any thoughts other than those of the fabulous woman he had met.

August 16, 1966,

During the course of the next two months, Bill hit the speed dial button with Judy's phone number dozens of times. Each time they spoke, she sounded cordial, even friendly, but he heard no hint of the fire they had shared that night in Atlanta. She politely declined several invitations to meet, citing a hectic schedule that kept her too busy to get away.

Bill refused to give up, determined to see her again, to be with her again. Then, unexpectedly, an opportunity presented itself on a September afternoon when Bill found he had to travel to Denver on business the following week. He immediately phoned Judy.

"Listen, I'm going to be in Denver next week," he told her. "Can we get together?"

"Bill, I told you I don't want you flying out here to see me," Judy said. Then, Bill heard a muffled "No, that's the wrong one" as Judy spoke to someone in her office.

"No, really, I have a business—"

"Just a minute, Bill," said Judy crisply and put him on hold.

Patiently, Bill hummed along with the music waiting for Judy to return. Three long minutes later, Judy finally came back on the line.

"Bill, I can't talk. Things are out of control here, and I've got to go."

"But, next week—Wednesday. Can we meet somewhere for dinner?"

He heard Judy's sigh. "Okay, we can have lunch. The Magnolia Café, in the old part of town. Eleven-thirty. Now, bye!"

When the day finally arrived, Bill simply radiated excitement, his happiness apparent to everyone around him. His indomitable cheerfulness and high spirits even invited curious stares from other passengers on his flight. On his arrival at Denver, he rented a car and, following the directions from the rental agency, drove into the city where he easily located the Magnolia

Café. He arrived shortly after 11 A.M., nearly half an hour prior to his scheduled rendezvous with Judy.

The Magnolia Café occupied a cozy nook within an old warehouse in the heart of downtown Denver's historic district. The warehouse had escaped the wrecking ball when a creative architectural design team sketched out a plan for boutiques, galleries, shops, and restaurants for the city block on which it sat. The old wooden walls and floors, the rustic tables, brass handrails, and soft lighting all conspired to give the place a warm, comfortable feel.

This is perfect, Bill thought, glancing appreciatively around the restaurant. He wondered if Judy had chosen this place for its intimate setting. He hoped so.

A hostess escorted Bill to the back of the room to a table nestled against a wall covered with photos of nineteenth-century Denver. Bill ordered a Scotch and water, then changed his mind and asked for a bottle of expensive Chardonnay, instead.

"Not even noon here," he thought. He didn't want Judy to think he was a regular drinker with the three-martini-lunch crowd.

Judy arrived at eleven-thirty on the dot. Spotting Bill waving to her, she made her way through the labyrinth of tables to join him.

Bill stood up to greet her, expecting Judy to simply extend a hand. To his surprise, she hugged him and gave him a small kiss on the cheek. Her touch sent the familiar electric shock down his spine.

"You're looking beautiful, gorgeous, exceptional—lovelier than ever." The words tumbled out of Bill, and he smiled self-consciously. "How are you?"

"You always know how to make a woman feel attractive, don't you?" Judy said wryly. "But, thank you. I'm doing fine. Just been busy as hell lately. How about you?"

"I'm doing great—now," Bill said. "Happy to be here with you." He pulled out Judy's chair for her to sit down. "Hope you're hungry. How about a glass of wine?"

"Yes, thanks. I usually don't eat lunch, but today I'll spurge. They have great salads here."

Bill signaled for the waitress. Judy ordered a Caesar salad topped with grilled chicken, while Bill opted for his perennial favorite, a French dip sandwich. The waitress poured them each a glass of the Chardonnay.

"So what brings you to Denver?" Judy asked. "Do you really have an appointment here?"

Bill raised his right hand as though taking an oath. "I do, scout's honor. I know you think I probably arranged it to give me an excuse to see you, but for years Wilson Industries has done quite a bit of business with a shipping company here. I'm meeting with the owner at three this afternoon. Whether I go back to Louisiana this evening or stay over and return tomorrow depends on how you answer my question."

"And what question is that?"

Instead of answering, Bill reached for his wine glass. "First a toast. Here's to you: It's wonderful to see you again." He clinked Judy's wine glass.

Judy's azure blue eyes stared back into his, her gaze friendly yet penetrating.

"Nice to see you, too," she said noncommittally.

They chatted easily about his work, her schedule, the cotton industry, and Denver's Indian summer weather until their food arrived. Judy drizzled honey mustard dressing over her salad, and Bill lustily dunked his man-sized sandwich in the plentiful sauce.

"Can you discuss business while you eat?" Bill asked playfully, refilling their wine glasses.

"Seems like I rarely have a meal where I *don't* discuss business," Judy answered.

"Good. I want you to listen very carefully to me. And please let me finish before you give me your answer. You're well aware that you've been on my mind constantly since we met in June. I've wanted very much to see you, but you've been too busy. At least, that's what you've said, and I hope it's the truth, because I can understand and appreciate that. However, I want to make you an offer.

"I need an administrative person to work with me full-time at Wilson Industries." Seeing Judy's incredulous expression, Bill held up his hand to stop her from speaking. "I know what your initial reaction to that will be, so let me assure you that this is a legitimate employment offer. I really do need someone with your talent and organizational skills. I've been lucky so far in managing my part of the company business, but I've gotten away with it primarily because of some very good people I've hired in key positions. Hell, I know my reputation for having floated through the company business. But as I assume more of the responsibility for running the whole show, I'm going to need someone like you in an administrative position. The truth is, I already need that person. I've just been postponing the decision to hire someone.

"The job will come with a car, a generous expense account, great health benefits, and a salary that beats what you're being paid now. And I'll also throw in something in your case that I wouldn't offer someone else. If you accept the position, I'll include a furnished condo in your own name.

"So, that's it. Everything's on the table." Bill picked up his wine glass and sat back, clearly pleased with himself. "What do you say?"

Judy put down her fork and pushed the half-finished plate of salad away. She turned her piercing gaze on Bill.

"You came all the way to Denver to ask me to be your mistress?" she asked icily. "You can sugarcoat it all you want, but essentially it's an offer to be kept by you, to be on call for you whenever you'd like 'a little company.'"

Bill leaned forward, his brow wrinkled in dismay.

"Judy, listen to me," he said earnestly. "I know it sounds that way to you, but believe me, it's not. Yes, I'm extending the offer in hopes that something develops between us. I'm not denying that. But, please, don't think you'll ever be on call for me. Your private life will be your own, although God knows I want to be a part of it. But your job won't hinge on our having a relationship. We'll draw up a contract detailing the whole thing. You'll be expected to work at the same performance level as any other employee. In addition to being attracted to you, I honestly feel you're the absolute best person for this job. I'm not attaching any strings to the offer, no matter how it may sound. My father still keeps his finger on the pulse of the business, and I assure you, he wouldn't sit by and watch me bring in some playmate on the company payroll." Bill started to reach across the table to take Judy's hand but thought better of it. "Judy, I want you to come to work for Wilson Industries. You'd be an asset to the company, and I think it would be a great opportunity for you, too."

Judy stared down at the patterned tablecloth. Bill could see that some of the anger had faded and been replaced by doubt.

"Bill, we spent one night together," Judy said, looking up at him. "Admittedly, it was a wildly exciting night, but it was nothing more than a fling. For you to come here thinking there was something strong enough between us to uproot me from my home and my work is...is...well, it's just absurd. We hardly know each other. And no matter how aboveboard you try to make the offer sound, we both know there *would* be strings attached. I'm the only one who has a key to my apartment here in Denver. I intend for that to remain the case regardless of where I live and until I choose to change that.

"I understand now how my actions that night made you believe I felt something more," she continued. "I know I moved too quickly, but it was just that the moment in time seemed so perfect. The suite, the dinner, the wine, and you. Everything fell into place. What we did was right at that time and in that place. But we're back in the real world now, and regardless of what you might think, I don't normally act like that. I'm flattered that you would extend an offer like this, but I can't accept. It would be a mistake. Believe me, I've made a few mistakes in the past, and I'm trying to learn from them, not repeat them."

Bill, looking much like a scolded puppy, sat silently for a few moments. Then, he shrugged his shoulders and gave her a half smile.

"You know I'm in love with you," he said.

"Don't say that!" she snapped, her eyes flashing. Bill suddenly realized he had said the wrong thing. "That's a very important word to me, and I won't allow you to use it so glibly about an encounter like ours. Your saying something like that simply proves my point about what would happen in Louisiana."

"I can't help it," Bill countered. "What I feel isn't an infatuation, and what happened that night was much more than a passing fling to me. You're right when you say I don't know much about you. What I do know is that I desperately want to give that mutual attraction we felt a chance to become something special."

"Then let's just move at a more reasonable speed. You're attractive, successful, and appear to be a fun guy, reputation and all. If you want, we can see each other and find out who we really are. If something develops, that's fine. If not, we can shake hands and part as friends. That's all I can offer."

Bill smiled ruefully and shook his head.

"All right, fair enough," he said, then he reached into his coat pocket. "Even though you turned down my offer, I have something I'd like to give to you."

"No gifts," Judy said emphatically.

"This is something I wanted to give you as a thank you for having lunch with me and for hearing me out. That's all. Christmas is only three months away. Consider it an early present from Santa."

He pushed a polished wooden box across the table. Judy took one look at the box, then looked at Bill skeptically.

"Bill, I recognize that box," she said. "That's what a Rolex watch comes in. There is no way I can accept a Rolex from you."

"Yes, there is a way. Just accept it in the spirit in which it is given, with my appreciation and affection. Or, you can leave it here on the table." Bill's smile seemed to dare her to refuse his gift. "The busboy or the waitress will enjoy it in that case. I'm not taking it back."

Judy looked at the box, then at Bill, then back at the box. Slowly, she reached out and slid the box closer to her. As she raised the lid, she gave a little gasp, then gently lifted a lady's diamond Rolex out of the box.

"Oh, my God, it has my name engraved on the back!" Judy gave Bill a look of sheer exasperation. "You're pretty sure of yourself, aren't you?"

Bill simply continued to smile at her, letting his eyes tell her how he felt.

"So just how do I explain this to my friends?" Judy asked. "They know that none of the guys I date can afford something like this, and they certainly know that it's way beyond my means."

"Tell them anything you like," Bill replied amiably. "Tell them it's from a mysterious admirer or a long lost uncle."

"Life is just that easy for you, isn't it?" observed Judy with a shake of her head. "That's several thousand of dollars' worth of admiration."

"Perhaps now you understand how deeply I feel about you," said Bill, then noting Judy's look of alarm, he added, "Just accept it as a gift with no strings attached and no expectations. All I want is for you to have the pleasure of wearing it."

Judy put the watch on her wrist and closed the clasp. Then, she held it up, letting the light catch it at different angles, her eyes growing wide as the highlights glinted off the sparkling stones.

"It's absolutely gorgeous," she said, "and I will accept it with thanks—but only if you understand that it doesn't change my mind about moving to Louisiana to work for you." She waited for Bill's grudging nod. "I agree, there is a certain attraction between us. I *would* like to see you again when we can coordinate our schedules. But I'm committed to staying in Denver, at least for the time being."

"I can live with that," Bill said, a happy grin splashing across his face.

"Well, my new Rolex watch tells me that it's time to get back to my office. What time did you say your appointment is here in town?"

"Three o'clock," Bill said. He had hoped Judy would ask him to spend the night with her, but something told him that to push for such an invitation would be a tactical error. "There's a six o'clock flight back to Baton Rouge I guess I'll try to catch."

Bill signed his credit card chit, and then he and Judy rose together to leave. As they moved toward the door, navigating around the tables of chatting patrons, Bill could feel the other diners' eyes on them. Instinctively, he pressed his hand lightly, but proprietarily into the small of Judy's back.

Once outside, Judy turned to him.

"My office is just around the corner," she said, "so, this is goodbye…for now." She stood on tiptoe and kissed Bill on the cheek.

"Can I phone you soon to see when we might get together again?"

"Yes, do that," she said, "and thank you again for the lovely present. I will treasure it always."

"Thank you for the kiss," Bill said, squeezing Judy's hand. "That makes it an even swap."

Judy laughed. "You are crazy and impossible."

"Take good care," Bill said and reluctantly relinquished Judy's hand.

Judy walked down the street, heading east. As she rounded the corner, she gave a little wave and then disappeared. Bill stood there for some time, daydreaming. He had laid all his cards down. Now he could only hope.

Driving back to the airport, Bill felt a twinge of guilt about the white lies he had just told. In fact, it was his flight he had to catch at three o'clock. The meeting with the shipper had been canceled the day before.

December 31, 1966

The months of fall passed quickly. Bill made it a point to speak to Judy at least once every week by phone, but between her work travel and his hectic schedule, he had not found another opportunity to see her. Thinking about her occupied much of his waking hours now, and she often crept into his dreams. His obsession had become more evident to everyone around him. Even his father guessed that someone had captured Bill's attention, but since Bill still dated several different women, Eric dismissed the obsession as simply another instance of Bill's compulsive behavior and assumed it would soon pass.

The Christmas holidays arrived, and along with it came the seasonal slowdown at the Wilson cotton operation. Bill took advantage of this slack time to plan a getaway in which he hoped Judy would join him.

Back in Denver, Judy waded through the traditional round of holiday parties. The few men whom she dated, all on a casual basis, each vied to have her join them in entertaining their clients. She accepted an invitation from Jim, a financial planner whom she saw frequently, to attend a New Year's Eve party. An intelligent, interesting man, Jim had nothing of the adventurer in him. Purely a numbers' cruncher, Jim was perfectly suited for his job helping people invest wisely for retirement, home, college, or whatever their personal goals might be. He had done all the right things in prepping himself for a successful career, but he had no fire, no passion, and thus far, no wife. If the world were divided into engineers and poets, Jim would feel completely at home with the linear lifestyle of an engineer. Judy occasionally experienced a twinge of guilt about going out with him, knowing she would never feel a spark, but she eased her conscience by often picking up the check.

The Saturday before New Year's, Judy had just poured steaming mugs of coffee for her mother and father, who sat chatting at her kitchen counter. Living in nearby Aurora, Colorado, her parents often dropped by on weekend mornings to catch up on their daughter's life. As Judy rummaged around in her pantry for a box of sweetener, she heard the doorbell rang.

"I'll get that," her mother said. "You go ahead with what you're doing."

When her mother opened the front door, she found a deliveryman from a local florist standing there, his arms filled with long-stemmed red roses.

"Delivery for a Miss Freeman," he said.

"Oh my!" Judy's mother exclaimed. "Wait just a second."

Crossing the living room to the couch where her purse sat, she retrieved a dollar bill, then returned to the front door.

"Thank you very much," she said, exchanging the dollar for the bouquet of flowers.

"Thank you, ma'am," said the deliveryman, tipping his cap.

She closed the door and carried the fragrant roses into the kitchen.

"Looks like someone certainly has an admirer," she remarked, her eyes holding a hint of a question.

Judy turned from the pantry to see her mother peeking from behind the colorful arrangement. She broke into a huge smile.

"Oh, they're beautiful!" she exclaimed. "Let's put them in some water right away. Dad, will you look in that top cupboard for a vase?" she asked, pointing above the refrigerator.

"Read the note," her mother urged. "Aren't you dying to see who they're from?"

Extracting the note from amidst the dark green leaves, Judy opened it and quickly scanned the two short lines.

"'Wish I were with you this day. Love from Bill, with no strings,'" she read aloud, an embarrassed smile spreading across her face.

"And who is this guy who is falling for my daughter?" her father asked, handing a delicate, hand-blown glass vase to Judy.

"Just a guy I met a few months ago in Atlanta," she said. "Don't go getting any ideas. It's nothing serious."

"Your father sent me flowers a few times before we were married," her mother said, stirring creamer into her coffee. She gave her husband a sidelong glance. "After we were married, though, I can't say that I ever remember seeing that delivery man again."

"I may not have been too good at sending flowers, but I was damned good at everything else I did," her father declared with mock sternness, and they all laughed.

✳ ✳ ✳

On New Year's Eve, Jim picked up Judy about ten, then drove to a local club where they joined two other couples to ring in the New Year. Afterwards, the whole party moved to Chez Jardin, one of Denver's finer restaurants, for a late dinner. The atmosphere was fun and festive, as revelers at every table celebrated the arrival of nineteen hundred and sixty-seven.

A harried-looking tuxedo-clad waiter finally came by to take their orders. Judy ordered a petite filet and lobster tail combo. Jim chose the prime rib. Each couple also ordered a bottle of champagne.

"Did you see the price on your 'surf and turf'?" Jim whispered during a break in the conversation with his friends. "Outrageous what they charge here."

"It's New Year's Eve," Judy said. "Everybody jacks up the prices on this night."

"Maybe so, but I still don't enjoy being gouged," he said, then muttered, "I hope you enjoy it."

Judy gave Jim an appraising look then answered evenly, "I'm sure I will. But don't worry. This will be my treat tonight."

The rest of the evening disintegrated into one long, downhill slide for Judy. She made small talk with Jim and their friends, but her thoughts kept returning to one depressing question: Why was she spending the most romantic night of the year with someone she didn't care about? She vowed never to make that mistake again.

As the evening dragged on, she glanced at her Rolex more than once and each time was reminded of Bill. She remembered his ready smile, his renegade image and bad-boy reputation, their steamy night in Atlanta. She found herself wishing she were ringing in the new year with him.

It was nearly 3 A.M. when Jim delivered Judy to her doorstep. Slipping her key into the lock, she opened the door then turned to face him. Jim's eyebrows rose, a silent question as to why Judy apparently was not going to invite him in.

"Thanks for the evening, Jim," she said. "Sorry if I wasn't the life of the party. I didn't realize how tired I was. Happy new year."

"Are you sure you're okay?" he asked, concerned. "You seemed pretty far away tonight."

"Really, I'm just worn out and ready to crash," she said. "I'll talk to you later this week."

"Sure, okay. Good night and happy new year." Jim gave her a chaste kiss on the cheek, then ambled down the steps and back to his car.

Judy slept until almost noon on New Year's Day, getting up only to make a pot of coffee and fetch the newspaper. She was still reading in bed when the phone rang around two.

"Hello?"

"Happy new year," a deep male voice said. Bill's voice.

"Well, happy new year to you, too," she said, stretching out in bed and letting the paper slide onto the floor. "It's nice to hear from you. How are you?"

Bill sensed something different, a definite warm tone in her greeting that had been missing during his numerous other calls.

"Doing fine but wishing I were there," he said.

"Thanks much for the flowers the other day," Judy said. "They were beautiful and came at just the right time. You've been on my mind."

Bill's heart kicked into high gear.

"That's only fair," he said, "since you seem to be on my mind all the time. Any good thoughts?"

"Maybe," Judy purred coyly. Bill felt like he was once again talking to the girl who had spent the night with him in Atlanta.

"Listen," Bill said, "I'd like to see you next week. I'll be in Denver again for another meeting. Will you be in town?"

"When will you be here?"

"On Friday. I'm taking a late flight Thursday night and have a nine o'clock appointment Friday morning. I should be through by around eleven if you'd like to have lunch or dinner or both."

"Yes, I'll be in town, and it just so happens I'm free on Friday."

"Great! Want to meet again at the Magnolia?"

"You probably eat as often in restaurants as I do. Why don't you come here, and I'll cook lunch for us. Maybe I'll show you a little of the Mile High City in the afternoon."

"That sounds wonderful. I'll phone you on Thursday before I leave to get directions to your place. I can't wait to see you."

"Looking forward to it myself. Bye now."

Bill hung up the phone, then let out a roar of excitement. Not only did Judy sound warm and welcoming and interested in seeing him again, she had invited him for lunch at her home. After that, well, he would let her take the lead. It had worked in Atlanta; he hoped it would work just as well in Denver.

During the next two days, Judy found her mind preoccupied more and more with Bill. The thought of that wild, wonderful night in Atlanta brought a smile to her lips. The expensive watch on her wrist made her feel valued. She began to question why she was resisting Bill's advances. Here was a good-looking, exciting man successfully running a family business empire which he would someday own, who insisted he was crazy about her. She had no doubt Bill had left a string of broken hearts in his wake, but who among the men she dated came equipped with impeccable credentials? After all, the men she knew were all in their mid- to late thirties. They each had their faults and more than a little baggage in tow.

For the first time, Judy seriously considered the job offer Bill had made during their lunch date. Would a move to Louisiana to accept a position in his company be completely insane? Or could it be a great opportunity? After all, what did she have in Denver that would be devastating to leave behind? Many of her friends had married, and she had little in common with them any-more. She did have a few close single friends whom she would miss, but they would understand. As for romance, of the men she dated, Jim was probably the closest to her, but he had never lit a fire in her anywhere near what she had experienced with Bill. On New Year's Eve, the contrast between him and Bill had suddenly become painfully clear. In charm, looks, generosity, and excitement, Jim would never be Bill's equal.

And she had to consider what her career track would be if she stayed in her present job. Convention management and business-event planning were developing into a specialized niche with a bright future, but as an up-and-comer in the industry, Judy had to practically live on the road. Just how far could she go with her company? And would the time away from home put a fatal strain on any relationship she might develop? As her thirtieth birthday approached, she also wondered about starting a family. She hadn't missed having children up to this point, but neither did she want to wait too long to be a mother.

Still, she wondered whether she was overlooking the obvious consequences of Bill's proposed working relationship simply because she had no major light in her life at the moment. Would he respect the line he promised to draw between her professional life and her private time? Was he really as crazy about her as he professed, or was he just frustrated at his inability to reach the forbidden fruit, so tantalizing because it remained just out of his reach?

Judy pondered these questions as she lay in bed Thursday night, just hours before she would welcome Bill into her home. Perhaps then she would learn some of the answers.

January 6, 1967

Bill tossed his briefcase onto the back seat of the Lincoln he had rented Thursday night when he arrived at the Denver airport. He had concluded his business with the owners of the interstate trucking company he used to haul cotton from Texas farmers to the Wilson mills at Oakleigh earlier than expected. Negotiations had gone well, which had surprised him, since for the past two days his mind had been filled with nothing but images of Judy. Now, finally, he was on his way to her home.

He threaded his way through light traffic as he traveled across town and then out of the city proper following the directions Judy had given him. The state's superhighways had opened up residential subdivisions on the fringes of the metropolitan area, as people had begun inching away from the busy urban cores. Judy's apartment complex sat in one of Denver's burgeoning western suburbs, nestled up against the foothills of the mountains where the city's growth had been steadily creeping. At an intersection marked by the ubiquitous shopping center, Bill turned and followed the feeder street about a mile to the Mountain Shadows apartments. Ten minutes later, after driving through a sprawling complex with tennis courts, swimming pools, and over five hundred identical units, Bill finally located Judy's building.

A heavy snow had fallen the day after New Year's, and the roads, while plowed and cleared, still boasted some impressive drifts along their shoulders. The weather had remained intensely cold but dry, making driving less dangerous than Bill had anticipated. Turning into the parking lot attached to Judy's complex, Bill found a space directly in front of her building, Number 2700. He donned his overcoat as protection against the temperature, which at noontime, the warmest part of the day, hovered in the mid-twenties. He grabbed the bottle of red wine and the potted paper-white narcissus he had brought as a gift for her home, then bounded up the stairs to the second level and knocked on the door of Apartment 205.

Judy opened the door almost immediately, her face alight with a wide, warm smile. Her flashing white teeth shone bright against the deep tan of her face, which she had acquired on a recent outing on one of Colorado's ski slopes. Her long navy-blue sweater covered her hips, complemented by a dove-gray skirt cut just above her knees, showing off her shapely legs. She looked fit, healthy, and happy.

"Hi, there," she said. "You found it."

"You give good directions," Bill replied. He entered the apartment and gave Judy a somewhat awkward hug, as he still held the wine and the plant. Judy, however, had nothing to restrain her, and she held the hug much longer than he had expected before she stepped back to look at him.

"What's all this?" she asked.

"Not yet," Bill said. "I'm still admiring the view. You look great."

"And who said 'Flattery will get you nowhere'?" Judy laughed. "Actually, I feel a bit frazzled. It's been a hectic morning, and I was late getting back here to start lunch. I barely had time to get ready."

"You did great," Bill said. He handed her the plant and bottle of wine. "I've really missed you."

"Well, it's good to see you, too." She set down the gifts and helped Bill remove his overcoat. "And what a beautiful plant—I love paper-whites!"

"Just a humble hostess gift," Bill explained. "We Southern boys don't believe in going to someone's home for the first time without bringing a gift."

"That is so sweet," Judy said, and to Bill's delight, gave him another hug and a kiss on the cheek.. "Make yourself at home," she said as she hung up his coat. "Lunch is almost ready."

Bill went into the living room, tastefully decorated with a leather sofa, love seat, and recliner. Several books lay scattered on an antique butler's table. A sliding glass door opened on to a balcony offering a panoramic view of the mountains to the west. In the far corner of the room, a plush, white flokati rug lay in front of a gas fireplace.

"Wow, this place is beautiful, Judy," Bill said, looking around, his appreciation genuine. "How long have you lived here?"

"I moved in shortly after they opened almost two years ago," said Judy, inserting a corkscrew into the top of the wine Bill had brought. "I enjoy it—when I'm here. Lately, that hasn't been too often. As you know, I've been doing a lot of traveling with my job." With a soft pop, the cork slid neatly out of the bottle. Judy filled two crystal wine glasses and handed one to Bill. "Come on, let's sit down for a bit."

Judy gestured at the sofa where they sat down, facing each other.

"You don't like all that traveling?" asked Bill.

"Oh, it just gets old—staying in cookie-cutter hotel rooms, being shoe-horned like a sardine in coach class." She gave his arm a little stab. "You know what it's like. Don't tell me you enjoyed your flight out here?"

"Well, it did give me a lot of time to think," Bill confessed.

"About what?" she asked.

"Three guesses," Bill said. He raised his glass. "It's great to see you again," he said, his eyes riveted on hers.

Judy clinked his glass with hers. "Well, it's nice to be seen," she said lightheartedly. She didn't flinch under his gaze, but held it, her piercing blue eyes sending the predictable searing heat down his spine.

Bill felt his heart kick into gear, but knew this wasn't the time to make a play. To keep cool, he took a long sip of wine then asked, "So tell me what's been happening."

"Well," Judy began, "I've been pretty busy. I hit the ground running with the new year. This is a pretty busy time for my business. We're getting ready for the round of spring conferences and meetings, outlining the summer programs, and seeing what lies ahead for the fall." Judy set down her wine glass and again fixed that penetrating blue gaze on him. "To be quite honest with you, I've been thinking about the job offer you made the last time you were in Denver."

Bill felt his involuntary intake of breath.

"Really?" he asked, trying to keep the eagerness out of his voice.

"I'd like to find out more about it while you're here." She smiled the smile he found so irresistible. "So, you see, that old adage is true."

"What old adage?" asked Bill, perplexed.

"The one that says 'There's no such thing as a free lunch.'"

Bill let out a hearty laugh.

"Baby, just name your price!" he whooped, then said, "Seriously, there's nothing I'd like better than to talk about what we're doing at Wilson Industries and how you'd fit in. The offer is still on the table."

Judy arose and moved into the kitchen, where she grabbed an apron off a hook and slipped it over her head.

"Great," she said, deftly tying the ties behind her back. "You can talk about it while I finish preparing our lunch."

"Need any help?" Bill asked.

"No, no, just relax right there and tell me more about—what did you call it, Oakleaf?"

"Oakleigh. Well, it's a long story, so I'd better get comfortable. Do you mind?" Bill stood up and began to remove his suit jacket, a questioning look in his eyes. When Judy nodded her okay, he slid it off and placed it over the arm of the couch, then loosened the knot in his tie. As he talked about life at Oakleigh, he marveled at how at ease he felt talking to Judy about business, his personal life, and anything else she wanted to know about him.

Fifteen minutes later, Judy interrupted him. "Lunch is ready. Would you like to help me set the table?"

Bill willingly obliged, then at Judy's request, opened another bottle of wine. Judy brought out two plates filled with chicken in a light cream sauce accompanied by pasta primavera, and they sat down to enjoy lunch and each other.

By two o'clock, they had finished their dessert of chocolate-dipped strawberries and were still lingering over their last glass of wine.

"When are you flying back to Baton Rouge?" Judy asked casually.

"I haven't decided," Bill said. "I wanted to be available to spend time with you."

"Good. Why don't we take a drive around Denver, then, and take in some of the local sights?"

"Sounds great. But, first, let me help you clean up here. That's the least I can do to thank you for that fabulous meal."

For the next several minutes, Bill took direction from Judy as they cleared the table, put away the food, and loaded the dishwasher. He enjoyed bustling around in her kitchen, feeling companionable and close to her.

When all was in order, Judy grabbed a full-length black leather coat from her closet and donned a white, fuzzy-knit hat. As she stood in front of her hallway mirror adjusting her cap so that her blonde hair cascaded attractively from beneath it, Bill watched, mesmerized.

"You look like something from *Dr. Zhivago*," he said.

Judy laughed. "Hey, it's cold out here," she said. "We're not in Louisiana, you know. It will be in the single digits tonight."

Interpreting this comment to mean that their afternoon drive would lead to dinner or some other plans for the evening, Bill let a grin spread across his face.

Judy insisted on driving since she knew where she wanted to take them, and Bill gladly consented. She led him down to the parking garage and to a late-model, Toyota. They began their tour in the foothills surrounding Judy's apartment, then made their way toward Denver, arriving just as the western mountains swallowed the setting sun.

Judy pulled into the parking deck and cut the engine. "What do you say we explore a little bit of downtown on foot?"

"I'm game," said Bill. When he opened the door, however, he was met by a blast of bitterly cold air. Though only a little before five, the pale twilight that had replaced the sun brought with it an icy finger of wind that sliced its way through their coats. After ten minutes of briskly walking the Denver streets, they gladly ducked into a noisy Irish pub, obviously a popular watering hole for the after-work crowd. A legion of pinstriped and button-down types crowded the bar, while waiters and waitresses in emerald green vests and bow ties served customers snuggled into wooden booths around the perimeter of the establishment. Huge picture windows fronting the busy street provided an ever-changing scene of downtown pedestrians scurrying along the sidewalks. Bill snagged a small table in the corner and gave an order for two martinis to a passing waitress.

"Let's talk a bit more about your job offer," Judy said, after the drinks had arrived. Bill had let Judy take the lead on this subject, not wanting to make her feel pressured. As he continued to explain his proposal for Judy's position in his business empire, she occasionally interrupted to ask a question. With each answer she searched his face for any sign of misrepresentation or a hidden meaning. A couple of martinis into the conversation, she found herself leaning toward accepting the offer. Was she feeling more comfortable with the prospects of accepting the offer and making the move, or was she simply trying to convince herself that she felt that way? At this point, she didn't know.

While she wasn't ready to accept the job just yet, she did accept Bill's offer of dinner. After he paid their tab to the waitress, they emerged into the wintry air for the two-block walk to Baxter's. One of Denver's premier steakhouses, Baxter's sat amidst a cluster of new office buildings that had transformed downtown Denver's skyline into a series of soaring glass and concrete peaks that rivaled those of the mountains just west of the city.

The cozy warmth of the restaurant offered immediate relief from the arctic cold that had chilled them during the short walk. A tuxedo-clad maitre d' ushered them to a booth set in a far corner of one of the dining rooms close to a blazing fireplace. A waiter immediately appeared, and Judy ordered another martini while Bill asked for a Scotch.

Bill continued to expound, almost playfully, on the virtues of living at Oakleigh and working at Wilson Industries. The more she heard, the more attractive the idea sounded. Searching for reasons compelling her to remain in Denver, she kept coming up empty.

When the waiter returned with their drinks, Bill ordered the house specialty of prime rib, while Judy asked for the filet and lobster tail.

"And some wine to go with your meal?" asked the waiter.

Bill handed the wine list back to the waiter without giving it a glance. "Just bring us your best bottle of Napa Valley Cabernet," he instructed.

The combination of a cozy fireplace, soft lighting, good wine, and Judy's company had given Bill a warm glow. Their conversation sprang spontaneously and ranged from politics to sports to travel to family and, of course, ever so often to the job proposal. Determined not to push, Bill would carefully answer each of Judy's questions, emphasizing the opportunity for her in making such a move. Judy seemed more and more receptive to the idea, and Bill let himself hope that the trophy he had pursued so diligently might finally be within his grasp.

If they had imbibed a bit too much at dinner, the brisk walk back to Judy's car sobered them up. As they neared the turnoff for Judy's complex, Bill spied the sign for a well-know hotel chain attached to the shopping center, and he shifted the conversation to the sleeping arrangements.

"Listen, Judy," he began, "do you have plans for this weekend? I don't have to be back at Oakleigh until Monday, and I'd like to see you tomorrow. Before you say 'yes' or 'no,' let me just tell you I plan to get a room tonight at the hotel here. I don't want you to think I came up here with any expectations other than seeing you and again extending the offer to join us at Wilson Industries. I enjoyed everything we did today—the lunch, the tour of Denver, the dinner, just seeing you again. I would love to take you up somewhere into your mountains tomorrow and find a chalet with a view and a fireplace.

Maybe you can even get me on a ski slope for a couple of hours. What do you say?"

In spite of herself, Judy was impressed. She had expected Bill to ask to stay at her house, and she hadn't been sure how she would have handled the situation. Relieved at his suggestion that they continue the platonic tone of their day together, she found the idea of meeting again the next day more attractive.

"Based on the lightning speed with which we kicked off this relationship back in Atlanta, I appreciate your slower testing of the waters," she said. "Tomorrow sounds like fun. I know a place we can go that I think you'll like. The weather should be perfect for a day on the slopes, so we can see if you have any potential as a medallist in the next winter Olympics."

Judy turned into the parking garage, glided the Toyota into her space, and cut the engine.

"It was a lovely day," she said.

"Thank you for all of it," Bill said. He leaned over and kissed her lightly on the lips. Sensing her quickened breathing, he pulled her close to him and their lips met for a long, lingering kiss. As they broke apart, Judy gazed into his eyes with that deep, inquisitive look that had come to define her. Despite the thrill of the moment, Bill pulled away and opened his door. Judy, smiling to herself, retrieved her keys and stepped out of the Toyota.

Bill took Judy's hand and held it firmly as they walked up the stairs to her apartment.

"Would you like to come in for a nightcap?" she asked, as she inserted her key into the door.

"Thanks, but I think I'll call it a night. I'm going to do a little paperwork and call it an evening, especially if you're going to haul me up to some ski slope tomorrow." He put his arms around her waist. "Thanks for a wonderful day. Shall I come by for you around eight? We can get some breakfast on the way out of town."

"Sounds great," Judy said. "I'll see you tomorrow."

Leaning down, Bill gave her another long, breathless kiss.

"Although this is good night for now," Bill whispered, "I know I'll see you in my dreams."

And with that, he turned and walked down the stairs without a backward glance.

January 7, 1967

Bill spent a restless night processing the images of the day and reflecting on how interested Judy seemed about the move to Louisiana and the job at Wilson Industries. The next morning, he bounced out of bed before the alarm rang and dressed quickly, eager to get to Judy's and see if she might be any closer to accepting the job. He had his sights set on this woman, and Bill Wilson rarely failed to acquire the object of his attention.

The icy air nipped at his nose the moment Bill stuck his head out the door of his hotel room. Drawing his overcoat tightly around him, he pulled the door shut and walked across the parking lot to his rental car.

I doubt I could live in a place with winters like this, he thought. Why, in a few weeks, Louisiana will erupt into spring flowers while the Rocky Mountains will be locked in winter for several more months.

When he rang the bell to Judy's apartment, she opened the door almost immediately, ready to go. They loaded her skis and poles onto the ski rack sitting atop her Toyota, and Judy tossed a bag with her ski boots and extra clothing in the back seat. After stopping to pick up some coffee and bagels to go at a crowded deli in the shopping center, they joined the weekend traffic on the highway, heading for the ski centers that had sprung up in the mountains just west of Denver.

"So, have you ever actually skied before?" asked Judy, biting into a cheese bagel Bill had smothered with herbed cream cheese and handed to her.

"I've taken a few lessons—you know, just the basics. I've never skied on mountains this big, though."

"Well, we'll just see what we have to work with," Judy replied, her side-long glance showing her amusement.

As they traveled through a number of ski areas without stopping, Judy explained that the closest resorts to Denver would be the most crowded.

They continued west through Loveland Pass and the towns of Dillon and Frisco before stopping at Breckenridge.

"The first thing we've got to do is get you the right gear," said Judy, pulling into a parking spot in front of a large building with "Rocky Mountain Outfitters" emblazoned on its marquee. "We can do one-stop shopping at this place."

Judy guided Bill through the ski shop, helping him pick out a parka, ski pants, a heavy sweater, wool socks, waterproof gloves, and a stylish knitted cap. Next, they moved on to the rental side of the store, where Bill was fitted for a set of skis, boots, and poles. As Bill emerged from the dressing room looking like a model for expensive ski apparel, Judy raised her eyebrows in approval.

"Well, you certainly look the part," she said. "Ready to go?"

"Just one more thing," replied Bill, walking over to a kiosk filled with sunglasses of all sizes, shapes, and styles. After trying on a few, he picked out a pair of mirrored wrap-around glasses, paying the exorbitant price without comment. Then he turned to Judy and flashed a winning smile.

"Now I'm ready."

They drove the short distance to the parking lot that sat at the base of a ski lift. After buying all-day ski passes, they rode the lift to the top of a beginner run that snaked down a gentle hillside flanked by stark aspen and evergreen trees. Bill did surprisingly well, considering how little he had skied in the past. Judy dutifully stayed nearby and offered pointers and encouragement—especially when he took a tumble. By one o'clock, they were ready for a break and some comfort food.

Judy led Bill to a mid-mountain lodge that sported a surprisingly large cafeteria. From the wide array of selections, they selected hot soup, sandwiches, and two mugs of hot buttered rum. Trays in hand, they made their way through the lunch crowd to the outside deck where the bracing air was tempered by the unfiltered sunshine. Unlacing their boots, they sat back and enjoyed a leisurely lunch while watching a legion of skiers wind their way down the mountainside.

After lunch, they made a dozen or so more runs, this time on more challenging slopes, before calling it a day. Although in reasonably good shape from his weekly routine at a gym in Plaquemine, Bill knew that the few hours they had spent skiing would reacquaint him with leg muscles he had long forgotten.

After returning Bill's rental equipment, they stopped into a Swiss chalet-style pub for a sundown cocktail. They decided on a bottle of red wine and a tray of appetizers to hold them until they could have dinner back in Denver. Conversation centered around the job offer again and what Judy could expect in the way of living arrangements. She seemed more and more interested in the opportunity, and Bill's excitement and enthusiasm mounted.

It was nearly seven by the time they began the two-hour drive back to Denver and a late dinner. Rather than stopping to change, they decided to go just as they were to a cowboy bar near Judy's apartment. A hostess dressed in Wild West garb escorted them to a table. When the waitress, decked out like a rhinestone cowgirl, arrived to take their orders, Judy convinced Bill to join her in ordering the house specialty—a combination plate of barbecued pork, beef, and chicken with side orders of baked beans and cole slaw. When they finished, Judy excused herself, ostensibly to visit the ladies' room. Instead she met with the waitress at the cash register and paid their tab. After Judy returned to the table, Bill flagged down the waitress and asked for the bill.

"It's all taken care of, sugar," she said, giving Bill a wink. "You have a nice night, now, y'hear?"

Bill turned to Judy. "You little sneak!" he protested. "I didn't want you to pay for dinner."

"Sorry," Judy smiled, "but it's already done. I don't want this whole day to be on you. After all, you're a guest here in Denver. You Southerners don't have a lock on hospitality, you know."

They drove back to Judy's apartment, and as Bill climbed out of the car, he could already feel the stiffness in his legs that would hobble him for the next couple of days. He walked slowly up the stairs with Judy's skis and poles, a pained expression on his face she couldn't help but notice.

"A little sore, maybe?" she asked, opening the door and taking the skis and poles from him.

"More than a little," he smiled. "My legs will remind me tomorrow how much fun I had today."

"How about a nightcap to celebrate the day?" Judy asked.

"I accept gladly."

Judy stashed her ski gear in a closet, then went into the kitchen to mix them a drink. Bill parked himself on the sofa.

"I hope you don't need any help," he said.

"Stay right there, rookie," she laughed. "What's your pleasure?"

"Whatever you're having," Bill said. "I won't have any problem going to sleep tonight. I didn't realize how tired I was until just now."

Judy fixed them each an Amaretto straight up in a snifter glass. She brought Bill his drink and joined him on the sofa.

"Here's to a great day," she offered.

"A wonderful day," Bill said looking deep into her eyes. They clinked their glasses and took a long pull on their drinks. Judy lit her first cigarette of the day and drew the smoke deep into her lungs.

"I guess it's terrible to suck in all that smoke and tar after breathing clean mountain air all day. But it feels pretty good just the same," she said. "Bill," she began, then hesitated, looking down into her glass as she swirled the amber-colored Amaretto. "I've given a lot of thought to your job offer."

Bill reached out and put a hand on her arm, the gesture of a friend rather than a lover.

"Judy, you don't need to give me an answer right now. Like I said, think about it for a while and let me know after you've had a chance to—"

"I'm ready to give it a try," she interrupted.

Stunned by her suddenness, Bill couldn't help but stare at her, shock registering on his face. He sat straight up on the couch, the exhaustion and aches of the ski day sloughing away instantly.

"You're surprised?" she asked.

"Well, no," he stammered, "just…just a little startled with…."

"With how quickly I made my decision?"

"I guess so."

"The more I thought about it, the more I couldn't find any compelling reasons for me to stay here. The move will mean a big change for me, but life *is* change. Nothing remains the same. I realize this is a huge opportunity for me professionally, and I'm excited about being a part of Wilson Industries."

Bill continued to stare at her, his mouth agape slightly. Then, shaking his head, he let out a hearty and delighted laugh.

"I'm thrilled!" he said. "I can't wait to get back to Oakleigh and put all this in place."

He placed his nearly empty glass on the coffee table.

"I think I'll take the morning flight back to Baton Rouge and get the ball rolling for your move," he said. "I'll call you when everything is just about ready. How much notice do you need to give your boss here?"

"I'd like to give them a month. I know they usually request only two weeks, but they've been very good to me. Thirty days should be ample time for me to train whomever they hire to replace me."

"That's perfect. It will take about that long for me to get everything ready for you at Oakleigh." He grabbed both of her hands. "Judy, I am so happy that you've made this decision. I want you to know that I am serious about making you very happy there. I hope you believe that."

"I do believe you," she said. "I believed you when you explained how this move will be a business arrangement. After I get there and start earning my keep, then we'll see if anything else develops. I'm looking at this job as a challenge—and a great opportunity to be a part of a growing company. All I can promise you is that I'll do my best."

"That's all anybody could ask," Bill said. "Listen, I'm going to head back to my hotel and get ready to fly out of here tomorrow morning. Thanks for a great day and making it even greater with your answer. Okay if I call you tomorrow before I leave?"

"Sure, I'll be here all morning."

Judy walked Bill to the door. He turned and drew her close to him, kissing her softly on each cheek.

"Thanks again," he said. "I'll call you tomorrow."

"Sleep tight," she whispered with a provocative smile.

"I will," said Bill, as he let her free of his embrace.

Bill drove the short distance back to the hotel, so excited he felt like celebrating. As he turned into the parking lot, he noticed the neon "Cocktails" sign flashing outside the hotel bar.

Well, if I'm going to sleep "tight," I'd better get a nightcap, he rationalized. I wonder if that cute little cocktail waitress in the lounge is working tonight.

Everyone at Wilson Industries agreed: Bill Wilson had turned into a completely different guy.

Ever since he'd returned from his trip to Denver, Bill had a bounce in his step, a gleam in his eye, a ready smile on his lips. He moved with a purpose few had witnessed before. He not only paid more attention to company business, he appeared to spend a good deal of time on some secret project that had piqued many of his coworkers' curiosity.

That secret project was Bill's logistical preparation for Judy's move to Wilson Industries. He had immersed himself in finding the right place for her to live, leasing a car, creating Judy's job description, and prepping his father for the addition of a new highly salaried position within the company.

After touring several homes on the real estate market, Bill had settled on a garden home in a new residential development on the outskirts of Plaquemine, which he bought in the company's name. Although he brought in an interior decorator to create a color scheme and arrange for the basic necessities, he knew Judy would want to complete the decor to suit her own tastes. One of Bill's poker buddies, a car salesman, gave him a good deal on leasing a new Cadillac, also in the company's name, for Judy's use.

Bill father's surprised him by asking very few questions about his creation of a new position—and a well-paid one at that—and bringing in someone from the outside to fill it. In the few conversations they had about it, Bill made the case that his workload had increased over the last several months and he was beginning to assume more responsibility and control in operating the business. When Bill explained who Judy was, Eric admitted to vaguely remembering meeting Judy at previous cotton grower conventions and functions. Bill felt certain, however, that the old man understood the underlying reason for bringing Judy on board. In fact, Eric made it clear that he would monitor the situation closely, especially in light of the fact that a home was being provided for the new employee. Eric knew all too well his son's reputation as a playboy, and he had no intention of footing the bill for some high-priced playmate.

By the time the moving date arrived, Bill had everything in place. The utilities were connected, the phone had been installed, and the car sat waiting in the driveway. He had arranged for any expenses and monthly bills to be sent directly to him. He had made sure he would be the one who had ultimate control.

Judy arrived on a bright and balmy Saturday morning in early March. Bill met her at the Baton Rouge Airport with a bouquet of long-stemmed yellow roses.

"Welcome to Baton Rouge," he said, giving her a hug, then thrusting the bouquet into her hands.

"Wow! Talk about a warm welcome!" Judy said. "These are gorgeous! And the weather! Did you arrange that too?"

"I'll only admit to doing what I can to make a good impression."

"Well, so far you've succeeded!" laughed Judy. She handed her carry-on to Bill. "Here, why don't you take this, and I'll carry the roses. People will think I'm some sort of celebrity!"

Bill looked down at the modest case in disbelief. "This is all you brought?"

"Well, the moving van with all my stuff is arriving tomorrow afternoon," explained Judy. "I didn't see any point in my lugging a bunch of clothes on the plane for just a couple of days."

Bill smiled. "Beautiful and practical. The perfect woman." He picked up the case and took her arm. "All right, Miss Freeman, your limousine awaits."

Bill pointed out landmarks and points of interest as they drove along the interstate to the town of Plaquemine. As they neared her street, Bill made Judy keep her eyes closed until he pulled up in front of her house.

"Okay, you can look now," Bill told her.

Slowly Judy opened her eyes and took in the scene before her: the stylish house, the tony neighborhood, the shiny, sexy, new Cadillac in the driveway.

"Bill...I'm...." She stopped, searching for a way to express how she felt. "Oh, Bill, this really is just so...well, it's all so wonderful!"

"Come on, let's go inside," said Bill, and he handed Judy her new house key.

As Judy walked through each room, she felt giddy with excitement and more than impressed with Bill's taste and the expense to which he had gone to provide such elegant furnishings. She decided she'd better put most of what little furniture she had brought with her in storage.

"Of course, it's not finished," Bill said. "I knew you'd want to do some of the decorating yourself—you know, make the place your own. I'll give you a company credit card you can use. You can buy whatever you like."

Judy just shook her head in amazement. Was she dreaming? This was all just too good to be true.

After Judy freshened up, Bill showed her around the town a bit to help her get her bearings. He took her past Oakleigh and Wilson Industries, giving her directions on how to drive there on her own. After stopping at the local supermarket to get a few things for her pantry and fridge, Bill returned Judy to her new home.

"Want to go out and celebrate your new life?" asked Bill.

"You know, I'm kind of overwhelmed by all this, and I'm pretty tired. I think I'd just like to have a quiet evening alone. I hope you don't mind."

"No, that's fine," said Bill, giving her a quick kiss on her cheek. "I'll check in with you tomorrow." Then, as if an afterthought, he kissed her again, this time on the mouth. "I am so glad you are here."

Judy smiled. "Me, too."

Bill made himself available to Judy for any help she might need during the next few days, which she had been given to complete her move before reporting to work. They had dinner together one night at a Cajun restaurant just outside Baton Rouge, but Bill was careful not to crowd her. He wanted her to become comfortable with the situation on her own terms.

When Judy reported for work, Bill had her officially briefed on the company by his secretary who also introduced her to the many department heads with whom she would come into contact in her capacity as Bill's administrative assistant. Bill remained noticeably on the sidelines during all this, well aware their relationship was the topic of many a water cooler conversation. Everyone clearly understood that Judy was to be considered the boss's main interest and off limits to anyone else.

For the next couple of months, the working relationship Bill had so urgently pitched to Judy proceeded as he had promised. Judy worked closely with Bill during the day, scheduling his appointments and coordinating his work activities. She quickly learned her duties and developed a sense of responsibility, often working late to ensure she had touched all the bases on a project. As had been her habit in every job she'd had, she did more than just what was expected of her.

Everyone she worked with, both within and outside the company, immediately recognized her ability and professionalism. Even his father praised Bill for bringing in Judy, once again acknowledging his son's knack for placing highly competent people in key situations. Still, Eric Wilson could not shake the feeling that his son had manipulated the situation for his own benefit, and he had every intention of continuing to keep an eye on events as they unfolded.

Bill and Judy went out occasionally, usually to a movie or to dinner. He always had her home at a decent hour and never suggested spending the night at her place. He assured her that she had the only key to her home, and he never stopped by unannounced. Despite the fact that he was still obsessed with Judy, Bill followed his game plan, determined to make her feel at ease and not rush the situation.

Eventually, an opportunity to move things along arose in June when Bill made arrangements for both of them to attend the annual cotton growers' conference, held this year in Memphis. On the second night of the conference, Bill and Judy made the rounds, visiting several hospitality suites and imbibing more than a few cocktails. As Bill walked her back to her room, he put his arm around her.

"You know I'm crazy about you," he whispered in her ear.

Judy stiffened, not sure she wanted to go where this was headed.

"Bill, I don't know if I'm ready for this," she heard herself say. Yet, she had to ask herself why she was hesitant. The working relationship was going well, and she certainly found Bill attractive.

"Judy, I certainly don't want to push you," said Bill, turning her to face him. "But you've got to admit I've been true to my word and kept everything kosher since your move. We've got a certain chemistry together, don't you think?" He put his finger under her chin and lifted her mouth to his, giving her a slow, sensuous kiss.

When they broke apart, Judy said nothing, but turned and continued down the hall to her door. Bill stared after her uncertainly as she unlocked the door and disappeared inside. Then, suddenly, she stuck her head around the door.

"Coming?" she called softly.

After Memphis, Judy felt a subtle shift in their arrangement. While Bill remained on his best behavior through the fall months, Judy realized that they were being inexorably drawn closer together. Though Bill still afforded her ample personal time alone and never assumed that he would stay over when they went out, still she couldn't shake the feeling that she was his possession. Yet each time her old feelings of apprehension arose, she quickly and firmly chased them away.

As the holidays approached, Bill and Judy found that the seasonal slowdown offered them considerably more free time, much of which they spent together. Judy had made several new friends, both male and female, but they all worked at Wilson Industries and kept a respectful distance. Bill supplied most of the entertainment in her life, but she couldn't complain. He planned weekend trips to Hot Springs, Arkansas, and Branson, Missouri, and picnics and bike rides along the levees that held back the lazy Mississippi River. Bill spent the night at Judy's more and more often, especially after the many holiday parties they attended that ran late into the night.

The Friday night before she was to fly to Denver to visit her parents for Christmas, Judy accepted a dinner invitation at Bill's parents' home. Judy knew Eric from work, of course, and had been a guest at Oakleigh for family gatherings, such as their annual Fourth of July barbecue and Thanksgiving dinner.

After dinner that Friday evening, everyone gathered around the Christmas tree in the great room to exchange gifts. Judy sat back and sipped her coffee, content simply to watch as Bill's mother and father distributed gifts to Bill, his sister and brother-in-law, Kristi and Steve, and their children, Misty and Jeff.

Bill then picked up a small box that had been hidden among the branches of the tree.

"This is something I got for Judy. I wanted all of you to be here when I gave it to her," he said. He handed Judy the small box wrapped in elegant silver-and-white-striped paper and accented by sheer silver ribbon.

Caught off guard, Judy flushed and put down her coffee cup, then took the present from Bill.

"Bill," she said, "I...I didn't think...I mean, I didn't bring anything for you," she said, her embarrassment obvious.

"Don't worry about that," said Bill. "Anyway, this gift is really for both of us."

Aware that all eyes in the room were on her, Judy slowly untied the ribbon and undid the wrapping paper. As she lifted the lid off the box, she gave a little gasp. Her hand trembling, she took out an exquisite diamond engagement ring set in a gold band and held it up for all to see.

Bill got down on one knee if front of her. "Judy, will you marry me?"

Judy stared at him, seemingly at a loss for words.

"Bill," she faltered, "it's beautiful. I just never...." Her voice trailed off.

No one spoke. Bill's father, Eric, and his mother, Debra, exchanged startled glances, each aware of the implications of Bill's proposal. Without any forewarning, he had invited this woman, whom they knew primarily on a professional basis, to become part of the family. Though Eric attempted to mask his feelings, Debra could see the concern in her husband's eyes.

Judy, uncomfortable at being the center of attention, smiled and tried to compose herself. Bill broke the silence.

"Remember when we met," Bill began, "and I told you I move quickly? Well, it's been almost a year since you decided to join Wilson Industries, and that's a lifetime for me. I've been patient, but I don't want to wait any more. I want you to be my wife."

A sudden icy feeling descended on Judy. While she was flattered to be proposed to by such an attractive, dynamic man—and to be asked to become part of such a wealthy and well-respected family—she felt manipulated by his making the proposal in front of the family without having broached the subject with her first. She knew he had engineered the time and place to make it difficult for her to turn him down.

"Please, Judy," Bill said again, "say that you will marry me."

Judy looked into the handsome face and heard herself say, "Yes, Bill, I will marry you."

Kristi, Steve, and the children rushed to hug and congratulate Judy, while Debra hugged her son and kissed his forehead. For several minutes, Eric stood slightly aloof, wearing a somewhat forced smile, lost within his own thoughts. Finally he went to Bill and shook his hand.

"You still have a knack for surprising the family, don't you, son?" he asked, an edge to his voice.

"I guess so, Dad, but for the first time, I thought this one through. It's what I want."

"Judy seemed somewhat surprised," observed Eric. "Had you discussed marriage with her?"

"We were meant to be together, Dad. Believe me, she's going to love being Mrs. Bill Wilson."

Bill walked across the room to Judy and pulled her away from the excited group of well-wishers.

"Is everything okay?" he asked. "You are sure about this, aren't you?"

"Yes, Bill, but I must tell you, I was shocked at how you did it. I mean, although we've become close in the last few months, we've never talked about marriage. You could at least have given me a chance to...."

"To what?" Bill asked. "Don't you want to be part of this? Judy, this company is on the verge of really taking off, and I will be at the helm. I want you by my side, to be my partner. You won't be an administrative assistant any longer, but one of the decision makers. My grandfather and my father built an empire here, and I'm going to take it to levels they never dreamed of. Now you'll be part of it, too."

Judy said nothing for a moment, digesting all Bill said. When she spoke, she chose her words carefully.

"I want to be your partner too, Bill, but to have a successful partnership we're going to have to have a lot better communication about major decisions than we had about this one," Judy said looking Bill straight in the eye.

Bill put his arms around her and squeezed her affectionately.

"Sure, honey. Whatever you say."

December 21, 1967

The holidays became a blur of activity for Judy. Back in Denver to visit her folks, she found the few days she spent there packed with the typical Christmas hustle and bustle. She also had several long talks with her parents, who were at first shocked and then dismayed at their daughter's decision to wed someone they had never met. Finally, Judy convinced them she had found happiness with Bill and had a great future with Wilson Industries, and they wished her the best.

On her return, Bill's parents held a small engagement party for them attended mostly by clients. Judy appreciated the gesture, relieved that his mother and father seemed to have warmed to the idea of welcoming her into the Wilson family.

When she brought up the subject of making wedding plans to Bill, Judy discovered that certain arrangements had already been decided.

"My sister had a huge affair with half of Iberville Parish here," Bill had informed her. "We don't need that kind of headache. I thought we'd just get a justice of the peace to marry us, then enjoy a wonderful honeymoon together."

"Do I have a say in this?" Judy had asked him, miffed at having been excluded from the decision making.

"Sure, honey, but I figured that since you had already walked down the aisle in a white dress once, you would be happy to skip some of the traditional formalities. Doing it this way makes it a lot less work for you. You wouldn't have to bother with booking a room, finding a caterer, sending out invitations—you know, doing all those things that drive people crazy. That's all right with you, isn't it?"

Taken aback by what Bill had said, Judy didn't answer for a moment. He had given this a lot of thought without once ever discussing his feelings with her. That feeling of foreboding she had felt on the day he proposed once again descended on her, but her more rational side took over. Maybe she was being overly sensitive about this issue, she thought. She decided to ignore the feeling and go along with Bill's plans.

"I guess that'll be okay," she said. "Whatever you think is best."

"Besides, I don't want to wait. Things are slow at work this month, so I think we should get married in a couple of weeks, then jet away to someplace warm and sunny in the Caribbean for our honeymoon."

Judy, unable to think of any reason why they should postpone taking their vows, agreed.

One rainy morning in late January, Bill and Judy drove to the judge's office in the Iberville Parish Courthouse. Without warning, Judy's sense of foreboding crept over her again, and this time it was harder to shake. Though she felt foolish, tears welled in her eyes and spilled down her cheeks. Looking over at her, Bill was startled to see her wiping her eyes.

"Honey, what's the matter?" he asked. "I hope those are tears of joy. You are happy, aren't you?"

She managed a smile. "Yes," she lied, desperately wishing she could shake the ominous feeling. Hoping to find solace, she reached over and squeezed Bill's hand. It was ice cold.

At the courthouse, Bill parked across the street, and he and Judy scampered through the rain and up the steps to the main lobby where Bill's parents, sister, and brother-in-law were already waiting for them. Judy's parents, both arthritis sufferers, had reluctantly declined their invitation, explaining that winter travel would be too difficult for them. They had called earlier that day to wish Judy and Bill well, and had promised to visit in the springtime.

After a brief round of hugs and kisses, Kristi handed Judy a bouquet and Steve put a boutonnière in Bill's lapel. Then the wedding party made their way to the office of Judge Robert Henderson. Eleven minutes later, they congratulated Mr. and Mrs. Bill Wilson on their marriage.

The honeymoon proved to be a welcome respite from the damp, gray gloom that marks winter in Louisiana. Bill and Judy flew to the Grand Cayman Islands, where Bill had rented a two-story villa for a week, complete with all the amenities and a breathtaking view. Each day brought soft tropical breezes and a new adventure. They walked and shopped along the famous Seven Mile Beach, strolled through the Queen Elizabeth Botanic Park with its garden trails full of blooming tropical splendors, took long soaks in the legendary mineral baths, and pursued all variety of water activities, of which scuba diving became their favorite.

Bill acted the part of the perfect attentive husband, seeing to Judy's every need. She began to relax and feel increasingly comfortable with her new position in life. She dismissed her earlier misgivings as ordinary wedding jitters.

However, uncertain feelings reappeared soon after they returned home. Without discussing it with her, Bill had arranged for a local moving company to go into Judy's house and move the few items she had collected to the huge antebellum home in which Bill lived on the family estate at Oakleigh. He had also put her house on the market, and it sold very shortly after it was listed. Of course, she knew that all of this would be done eventually; what bothered her was he had never said a word about any of it to her. She couldn't help but feel left out. After all, she was his wife now.

Over the next few weeks, the newlyweds settled into their routine. Bill, who had an office in one of the downstairs rooms of the two-story mansion, began spending more time there and less time at Wilson Industries corporate headquarters. Judy still went into work each morning and continued to earn the admiration of management and staff with her talent and ability, despite her new position as the boss's wife. Instead of this pleasing Bill, as it had in the past, any compliments about Judy and her work turned him surly, spawning what seemed to Judy like resentment or jealousy from her husband.

Bill also became more secretive with her in matters pertaining to the business. Instead of including her in the decision making, as he had promised when he proposed, Bill now excluded Judy more than ever. When she questioned him about it, he abruptly brushed her off, telling her not to meddle in his affairs. She also noticed his attitude carrying over to their after-work hours as well. He became moody, silent, and morose, often requiring days to get over incidents that only a year ago would have been insignificant. Judy saw a side of him that she hadn't known existed. A dark cloud seemed to have descended over him, transforming what should have been the happiest time in Judy's life into a period of questioning.

"Did all this happen too fast?" she had wondered. Had she been too easy a conquest for him? Was she partly to blame for his transformation after he had slid the ring on her finger? Had their marriage come to represent Bill's final acquisition of the missing piece to his life's puzzle, and once acquired, would it now become an irrelevant item to be added to the list of casual possessions for which Oakleigh was known?

Although Judy wondered about these questions, she didn't become overly concerned until Bill's temper started to emerge. Little by little, those minor problems that once sent him into his dark depression now led to violent eruptions that sometimes took on a frightening tone. When Judy would confront him the next day about his inappropriate behavior, he would apologize and blame his moods on the proposed business expansion plans weighing heavily on his mind. He promised to try harder to bring back the happiness that had once surrounded them.

The moods persisted, however, and became more frequent. Although she'd never found it easy to talk about personal matters with her new mother-in-law, Judy finally felt she needed to talk to someone about her marital problems. Over coffee one afternoon in the main house at Oakleigh, she confided in Mrs. Wilson.

"Debra," she began hesitantly, setting down her coffee cup. "I'm very concerned about my...about our marriage. It's...well, our relationship is...strained." She looked at her mother-in-law for any sign of sympathy or comfort. "For some reason, Bill's changed dramatically. He has terrible...I don't know...almost tantrums, where he becomes unreasonably angry, sometimes over the smallest thing. I've tried to talk to him about it, but he just says he won't do it again. But, so far, that hasn't worked."

Debra looked at Judy with disdain, her steel grey eyes holding no trace of womanly understanding.

"Never forget," she said, looking directly at Judy, "that as Bill's wife, you are part of the family, and the family is Wilson Industries. Nothing gets in the way of that."

Judy gave a little gasp, shocked at the cold, hard words of advice her mother-in-law had for her.

"Whatever is worrying Bill is no doubt a natural result of the pressures of his work. Wilson Industries is a huge company, one that requires an enormous amount of attention from the Wilson men. In turn, they depend on their women to fully support them without questioning their motives or tactics. That is your role now."

Judy wondered whether Debra Wilson had at some time in the past found herself in the same situation that Judy now faced. Perhaps she had struggled with these same feelings with Bill's father, Eric, after he had assumed the helm of the cotton empire from his own father. However, Judy had a hunch that the role of the genteel Southern belle standing beside or, preferably, behind her man had come easy to Debra, and she fully expected Judy to conform as well.

Judy said nothing more, but quickly finished her coffee and made her excuses to leave. She resolved never again to confide in her mother-in-law.

Judy and Bill fell into a livable but less-than-desirable routine. Although there were times Bill would be the light-hearted, devil-may-care man Judy had once found so appealing, more often he was emotionally unavailable to her. They began to drift apart. In public, they still presented a picture of the happy couple to maintain appearances, but that was clearly not the case at home. Although he gave Judy a very comfortable lifestyle and a prominent position in Baton Rouge society, Bill seemed uninterested in offering little else to the marriage. He became increasingly remote, spending long stretches alone in his office, a bottle of Scotch his usual companion. Judy told herself she was reasonably happy and that probably no marriage was perfect in every way. She also kept reminding herself that she might have been partly to blame by having been such an easy conquest for Bill.

Because of Bill's increasing aloofness, their mutual sexual chemistry had dwindled. However, many nights, he came to their bedroom more than a little drunk, crudely and almost frighteningly forcing himself on her. It was at those moments Judy found it most difficult to adhere to her mother-in-law's admonishments.

Still, Judy tried to brush off even these bumps on the matrimonial highway, until Bill grew increasingly and unreasonably jealous. What began as a barely noticeable irritation whenever Judy interacted with her male co-workers soon grew into fits of jealous rage. Instead of taking Judy to task, however, Bill secretly threatened any man she happened to speak to or work with. After a while, when Judy found that most of the men in the office avoided any kind of contact with her, she was sure she understood why.

The fits of jealousy soon mushroomed into a full-blown resentment and suspicion. Bill constantly asked her where she was going, what she would be doing, and who she'd be with. It didn't matter if she was just running to the supermarket or going to a nearby health club to meet one of her girlfriends for a workout. Judy had few close female friends, but even they became increasingly hesitant to spend time with her due to Bill's constant questioning and uncomfortable intrusions into their time together.

Judy eventually realized that Bill was steadily isolating her and forcing her to become more dependent on him. One day, he suggested she give up her position at the company. Judy firmly opposed the idea. Bill launched many an angry tirade over this issue, but Judy held her ground. Giving up her job would mean losing the last bit of freedom she felt she had, and she knew she must not allow that to happen. Finally, realizing how strongly she felt about this demand, Bill grudgingly gave up on the idea.

Judy never spoke to her parents about the deteriorating condition of her marriage. Her mother and father did make several pilgrimages to Oakleigh, usually in the spring, but Bill and his family always acted the part of the perfectly charming Southern hosts. However, her father, who always had a knack for reading Judy's unspoken thoughts, sensed an undercurrent of discontentment when he and Judy talked during their many walks around the grounds of the estate, but he said nothing.

Bill continued his moods swings. Sometimes he played the part of the perfect husband—charming, attentive, loving. But those occasions were sunny islands in a sea of dark behavior. More often he was sullen, increasingly withdrawn, and even verbally abusive. One night, when Judy confronted him about his moods, Bill responded with a litany of screaming expletives that left her shell-shocked. As he usually did after one of their arguments, Bill came to her later to apologize and promise to be a better husband in the future. Judy no longer allowed herself to hope he would keep his word

Married life became a series of lonely hours for Judy as Bill increasingly swung from withdrawn to confrontational, from stony silence to verbal attack. He also began traveling more, supposedly to meet with potential customers involved in his expansion plans for the business. Judy wondered if he was seeing someone else on his business trips and reverting to the "anybody and everybody" image that he had assured her he had outgrown before they were married. Judy immersed herself in her work as an outlet from the emotional wreckage that she felt at home.

A turning point came when the verbal abuse escalated into physical abuse as Bill began slapping Judy during his fits of anger. Afterwards, he would come and apologize, uttering his empty promises. But, finally, Judy had to climb out of her denial and accepted the truth. Her marriage had been a hasty decision to a man she had known little about. And what she knew now was frightening.

After almost two years of enduring an increasingly bad situation, Judy gathered her courage and knocked on the door to Bill's study.

"What?" came Bill's bark.

Judy opened the door to find Bill sitting in his black-leather desk chair, his back to her. "Bill, we need to talk."

Bill swiveled around, his face wearing an unfriendly scowl. He held a tumbler of Scotch in his hand.

"About what?" he snapped.

Judy moved over to the office's plush sofa and perched on an arm.

"Bill, this marriage is not working. You seem miserable and angry most of the time. I know I'm not happy. And...and you can't go on hitting me. I'm having a hard time hiding the bruises from people. I—"

Judy stopped abruptly as she watched Bill jump out of his chair and cross the room in two quick strides. He grabbed her shoulders and lifted her, shoving her up against the wall next to the sofa. He put his face close to hers, his whisky breath giving fire to his chilling words.

"You're a member of the Wilson family and of Oakleigh now," he screamed. "That will never ever change." Suddenly, his voice dropped to an ominous whisper. "You just better adjust to the situation and enjoy the financial rewards. You can try harder to be a better wife!"

With a malevolent look, he let go of Judy, who crumpled to the floor. Then he turned, grabbed his suit coat, and stormed out of his office. Judy heard the front door slam and his sports car roar as he sped off into the night.

Judy sat slumped on the floor, sobbing. She felt deeply alone and helpless, like a bird trapped in a cage. For the first time in her life, she felt afraid.

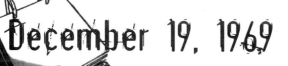

December 19, 1969

When December of 1969 rolled around, Bill and Judy attended the traditional round of Christmas parties, smiling politely and giving an outward appearance of a happy couple. Life at home, however, had settled into two people just sharing living quarters. Still, there were brief pockets of companionship, which gave Judy hope that their relationship would return to what it had been. They visited New Orleans on business several times and had a reasonably good time together. They even took a short cruise that fall back to the Caribbean, where they had spent their honeymoon. Bill had been on his best behavior, doing many of the little things he had done when courting Judy.

The first night on board, he stood in front of the door to their luxury suite and smiled down at Judy.

"Darling, things haven't been good between us for a while, but I promise I'll make them right." Unlocking the door, he impulsively turned to Judy, gathered her up in his arms, and carried her over the threshold of their room. As they entered, the intoxicating fragrance of dozens of lush tropical flowers inundated her.

Bill set Judy down on the sofa. A magnum of champagne sat in an enormous ice bucket, awaiting their attention. Bill popped the cork, and Judy giggled as the bubbly brew streamed down the sides of the huge bottle. As they drank the champagne, Judy began to feel giddy. Before she realized it, Bill picked her up from the sofa and carried her over to the bed, which he had strewn with a blanket of rose petals. Surprised, she willingly yielded to his every desire.

They made passionate love together for the first time in several months. Since the lovemaking had been unplanned, Judy had no means of contraception. Briefly the thought that she should take some precaution passed through her alcohol-induced euphoria, but she let her passion overrule caution.

Prior to their Caribbean pleasure cruise, Judy often wondered if having a child together would make a difference in their relationship. But every time she had broached the subject, Bill had refused to discuss it. And Bill's insistence that she wear a diaphragm whenever they made love gave a clear indication that children were not in his plans.

But in the Caribbean, Judy and Bill rediscovered that steamy, physical desire for each other, and Judy began to believe things would work out between them after all.

She was wrong. After returning to Oakleigh, the bright spots in their marriage were few and far between. Bill returned to his cyclical bouts of drinking, which inevitably led to verbal and physical abuse, followed by next-day apologies and promises to be a better husband. Unable to cope with this emotional merry-go-round, Judy began to distance herself from Bill as much as possible and, instead, turned her energy and focus on her job. They both made sure that, to all around them, all was well with their marriage.

Each year, the premier social event of the holiday season in Iberville Parish was the Christmas party thrown for the Wilson Industries employees. The entire Wilson clan hosted a lavish dinner at Oakleigh, complete with open bar, dancing, and the presentation of Christmas bonuses for the staff. This year the event would be even merrier, as the company's profits had soared during the last twelve months with the expansion into new markets both at home and abroad.

As a member of the Wilson clan, Judy helped stage the event and the Wilsons appreciated her efforts. She noticed that Bill's family seemed to be a little cozier towards her during the holidays, a departure from the distant, even chilly feeling she usually felt in their midst. This evening, the entire family appeared to be in good spirits, especially Bill who was doing a commendable job of presenting an image of a happy husband. He made the rounds with Judy, talking big about how his efforts that year had been responsible for Wilson Industries' prosperity—a boast few took seriously. Most understood that what Bill did at work was mostly for show. Although his father, Eric, had hoped to pass on the company to his son, he had found Bill to be erratic and ineffectual in his business dealings. Too shrewd to be sentimental, Eric remained the driving force behind the Wilson empire.

Bathed in the warmth of the holiday cheer, Judy decided the time was right to give Bill the news.

As the band played a slow, sultry tune, Judy took Bill's hand and led him on to the dance floor. For a brief moment, she closed her eyes and imagined herself with the man who had so excited her that first night in Atlanta.

"Bill," she whispered, "I have some news for you."

"What's that?" he asked.

"Remember when we were on the cruise in October, our first night as we sailed away to the Grand Cayman Islands?"

"Sure," he responded, still sounding puzzled.

"Well, that evening resulted in a very interesting event. We're going to become parents."

Bill stopped in his tracks. An astonished look came over his face. Then he took Judy's hand and walked her outside onto the patio overlooking the swimming pool.

"Judy," he said, his voice like ice, "that's out of the question.".

It was her turn to look astonished.

"What do you mean 'out of the question'?" she asked. "It's a fact. The doctor's office phoned me with the test results two days ago. We're going to have a baby in late May or early June. I was hoping you'd be pleased and that this might turn things around for us."

"Pleased? How could you think I would be pleased? How could you be so careless? Children are definitely not on my list of priorities right now. You see how busy I am with work. There are a lot of big things happening. I have to be able to travel on a moment's notice, maybe be gone for weeks at a time. I can't be tied down to a baby, for God's sake. It's totally out of the question."

"Bill, there is no 'question.' I'm pregnant with your baby, and we're going to be parents in a few months."

"That's not going to happen. You've got to get rid of it."

Judy began to burn. She was determined to speak her mind regardless of who heard them.

"Listen to me, Bill," she began, regaining her composure. "There's no 'getting rid' of anything. I'm going to have this baby, our baby, and you can accept that fact or not. If you want, you can divorce me. That's fine, too. I'll have the baby and raise it alone, but you…."

Bill seized her arms and gave her a violent shake. The rage in him showed on his face like a storm cloud.

"Don't ever mention divorce again," he seethed. "I'll never give you a divorce. Don't you know that? Haven't you learned anything in the two years you've been here? This family is too powerful in this state. You are and always will be my wife. Case closed. And I wasn't planning on having babies to…."

"You may not have planned it, but it happened. We were together that night on the ship for the first time in a long time. We may both regret it now, but the fact remains that we have conceived a child, and I'm going to have it."

Bill looked at her, his mouth curving into a leer. "Yeah, we haven't had much sex lately, have we? Hell, that baby might not even be mine."

Judy returned Bill's look, her eyes filled with disgust and anger.

"You bastard," she said. "I have no love at all in my heart for you right now. You can turn your back on me and on this child, but I'm going to have it and raise it and pray that it doesn't grow up to be like you!"

Bill's eyes returned her fury. "Get your coat," he ordered, abruptly turning to leave. "We're getting out of here."

Returning to the party, Bill and Judy made a perfunctory attempt at hasty goodbyes, citing everything from headaches to hectic schedules as the reason for their early departure. For once, however, everyone could see something was amiss.

They drove home in stony silence. Bill headed straight for his study. Judy went to bed. Even though she locked the bedroom door, Judy feared Bill might try to harm her and the baby. She didn't sleep much that night.

The next morning, Bill again offered one of his trademark apologies for his actions the night before. He explained his behavior to Judy by saying he had simply been caught unaware by the news and assured her he would be a model father. To prove it, he phoned his parents and sister to give them the good news.

Judy, however, was unmoved by Bill's rote apology. She was truly frightened. Somehow she would endure the situation, but from now on her marriage would be one in name only. Her job would be to protect and raise her baby.

In March, just as Judy was beginning to show, Bill's parents held a party to announce the impending arrival of the newest member of the Wilson family. They even flew Judy's parents down for the event. Judy's father immediately saw Judy's strained attempts at gaiety for what they were—a desperate effort to convince her family that she was happy.

At one point during the party, he took her aside.

"Judy, honey, you don't seem like yourself. You seem...I don't know...anxious," he said softly. "What's bothering you? Do you want to talk about it?"

Judy squeezed his hand and willed back the tears threatening to spill onto her cheeks.

"Oh, Dad," she said with a too-bright smile, "I'm fine. It's just that, I guess, being pregnant plays havoc with my hormones. I'm really very happy and looking forward to this baby."

She gave him a reassuring smile and then rejoined the party. She would have loved to tell him her troubles, to let him enfold her in his arms as he did when she was little. But she was determined to walk the road alone.

June 19, 1970 to September 6, 1978

On June 19, 1970, Judy gave birth to a seven-and-a-half pound healthy baby boy, Michael Thomas Wilson. The newest addition to the Wilson family favored his mother, with the same piercing blue eyes, blonde hair, and, as he grew older, an easy disposition.

For his son's first year or so, Bill became a bit more attentive as a husband and actually surprised Judy and the family with his attempts to be a good father as well. As the child grew older, however, Bill seemed to lose interest and drifted further apart from his wife and his son. He spent an increasing amount of time away from home on business trips and spent long hours at the company's offices. On weekends, he'd often make plans with his son, only to cancel at the last minute, usually using "company business" as an excuse. Unable to build a strong attachment to his dad, the child clung to Judy.

Judy found Bill's parents surprisingly supportive in helping raise their grandchild. But she never saw that overwhelming sense of love most grandparents characteristically show their grandchildren. Judy sensed that the family's attachment to Wilson Industries and their devotion to the growing empire overshadowed the importance of any individual member of the clan.

The situation at home became even cooler as young Michael grew. Judy had long ago moved into her own bedroom, and Bill rarely made nighttime visits to his wife's quarters. That didn't bother Judy; in fact, she preferred he kept his distance. Bill's lack of interest in her sexually convinced her he satisfied whatever needs he had with other women while on his frequent business trips. She had long ago stopped hoping for a marriage built on love. Instead, she made her sole purpose in life being a good mother to her son.

Mike, as he came to be called, grew into a bright young boy, a good student who did well in his studies. He had just started the third grade at the

Lafayette Christian School in nearby Plaquemine when Bill and Judy had an encounter that changed their lives forever.

Judy and Mike were returning home from an afternoon open house where Judy had met Mike's teacher for the new year. Judy had hoped Bill would accompany them, but he had gone out of town the day before.

"This is an important business meeting that just can't be postponed," Bill had insisted, silencing her protest.

As she turned onto their street, Judy saw Bill's car in their driveway. Irritation immediately flooded her. Surely he could've come to the school and at least said hello to the teacher, she had fumed inwardly.

Mike scampered up the stairs to change clothes, and Judy went into the kitchen to start dinner. She noticed the door to the laundry room had been left open, presumably by Bill, since she could see the clothes from his trip lying in a pile on the floor in front of the washing machine. Judy decided she'd get a load in before dinner and began sorting the whites from the darker colors. As she threw a shirt into the white pile, she frowned, then picked it up again, staring at what looked like red marks on the collar. Although they were faint, as if someone had tried to rinse them away, she knew them to be the unmistakable telltale signs of lipstick.

Judy dropped the shirt on the floor and went into the kitchen. She poured herself a glass of wine, then wearily sat down at the kitchen table.

A few minutes later Bill came in, having just showered and changed into sport clothes.

"Hi," he said.

Judy didn't answer.

"What's the matter?" Bill asked.

Judy took a sip of her wine.

"You don't have time to attend the open house to meet your son's new teacher, but you do have time to screw around on the road," she said looking down at her wine.

Bill walked over to Judy and stood directly in front of her. When she looked up at him, Bill slapped her hard across the face. Slowly she turned back to face him, blood trickling from her nose. Her head throbbed, but she'd be damned if she'd give him the satisfaction of seeing her cry.

"Don't you ever tell me how to live my life," he said, his voice low and threatening.

Judy stood and walked over to the kitchen counter where she tore a paper towel from the rack and held it to her nose.

"You must be very proud of yourself," she said. "That's the first time you've ever drawn blood. I promise you it will be the last."

Bill sneered insolently, then turned to walk to the wet bar to pour himself a Scotch. That's when they both noticed Mike standing in the doorway.

"Dad," he cried, "why did you hit Mom?"

"Go to your room, Mike," Bill said angrily. "Now!"

Judy got up and went to her son.

"It's okay, honey; I'm all right. Go out into the back yard."

Hesitating as he looked from one parent to the other, Mike did as his mother asked. Judy watched him walk across the back yard and into the garage. In a moment, he came back out with his bicycle, which he jumped on and then sped down the driveway and into the street.

Judy turned back to Bill.

"You bastard!" she said. "Does that make you feel like a man? Hitting me in front of our son? How long will it be before you start hitting him? You may have ruined my life, but I'm not going to let you ruin his." Trembling, she fought to gain control. "It's over, Bill. Do you hear me? I'm going to meet with an attorney as soon as I can and file for divorce. You can do whatever the hell you want to do."

Bill laughed mirthlessly and lifted his glass as if in salute. "Good luck. You'll never find a judge in Iberville Parish who will give you a divorce."

"We'll see," Judy said. "I don't know what's out there, but I do know that anything is better than this lie we've been living. I should have done this long ago, but I thought keeping the family together would be the best thing for Mike. I know now that was a mistake, the worst decision I ever made— next to agreeing to marry you. I've shielded Mike from the abuse all these years, but you fixed that today. Now he knows, and I don't have to pretend anymore. You have your choice. You can leave or Mike and I will leave, but I won't stay with you a moment longer."

An eerie calm seemed to have settled over Bill.

"I'm leaving tomorrow morning for meetings in Las Vegas," he said, then added indifferently, "Do what you want."

"I don't want you coming back to this house," Judy said. "If you do, Mike and I will leave. I won't stay under the same roof with you."

"Suit yourself," Bill said. "I'll move into one of the guest houses on the grounds when I get back."

Bill finished his Scotch, packed another bag, and left the house without saying another word.

Judy, glad for the opportunity to be alone, began making plans. She phoned Barbara, the only person she considered to be a close friend and confidante to tell her what had happened. Barbara was not surprised. She had sensed for a long time that things were deteriorating in Judy's marriage even though she had not asked Judy about it. She invited Judy and Mike to stay with her, but Judy declined, saying that Bill had left for a trip and would be moving out when he returned home.

Barbara also suggested an attorney Judy could call for a consultation on her divorce plans. Judy took the number and thanked Barbara, promising to keep her posted.

"Judy," Barbara said, "are you at all frightened? You know what a temper Bill has and how his drinking affects him. The Wilson name can buy him a lot of leeway with these Louisiana police, both the local cops and the state. If you feel at risk at all, you need to—"

"I'm fine," Judy interrupted. "I was a bit shaky, but I've cleared my head, and I've got a plan of action, thanks to you."

"Be careful," Barbara cautioned. "And call me if I can do anything—anything, you hear?"

The next morning, Judy phoned the office of Alex Thibodeaux, the attorney Barbara had recommended, and scheduled a 1 P.M. meeting the next day at his office in Plaquemine.

"Judy, you must know this is going to be a long and dirty fight," he told her after listening for almost an hour to her story. "You're not only taking on Bill, but the entire Wilson empire. If it comes down to a courtroom with a jury, there will be a hoard of press and media attention. I'll agree to take this case only if you are one hundred percent certain that reconciliation is out of the question. If you commit to going through with the divorce proceedings, you'll be in it for the long haul."

"My mind is made up," Judy said. "It's over between us, and I want to cut all the strings."

"Before serving him with papers, you'll want to have concrete evidence about his infidelity. That will mean private investigators, photographs, taped telephone conversations, the works. Since you've told him already that you plan to leave him, he'll probably be much more circumspect about any involvements he has. And the other side will no doubt try to drag you through the mud."

"I don't care. I've got nothing to hide, other than putting up with his abuse for all these years. I'm not proud of that. I should have done this a long time ago. I just kept on hoping…well, you're a divorce lawyer; you know the story. Anyway, I'm ready to go through with it now. Tell me what I need to do."

"I'll handle the details. I'll call a private investigator I often use, Walter Angelle. He's very good at his job, and he's discreet. I'll ask him to come out to see you tomorrow to talk to you about putting a device on your telephone."

"But Bill's moving to one of the guest houses," protested Judy. "He won't be using the phone in our house."

"Do you have access to the guest house he'll be staying in?" asked the lawyer.

Judy shook her head. "I'm not even sure which one it'll be. There are four on the grounds."

"Well, we'll put one on your phone anyway. Who knows? Maybe one of his women friends will try to contact him at your house. It's worth a try. And, Judy, tonight I want you to jot down anything you can think of about Bill's behavior and travel patterns, anything at all that might help your case. The investigator will want to interview you to get all the information on Bill he can."

"Good," Judy said with more confidence than she felt. "I'm ready to move forward right away."

The next afternoon, the private investigator arrived and interviewed Judy, spending over two hours asking her all kinds of questions. Before he left, he installed a listening and recording device on Judy's phone. Although Judy felt uncomfortable about the whole procedure, she knew it was probably just the first in what would be a long list of uncomfortable situations in which she would find herself in the coming months.

Two days later, Bill's mother, Debra, suffered a massive stroke. Bill cut his road trip short and went right from the airport to Sacred Heart Hospital in Plaquemine where he met his father, sister, and Judy.

Bill hugged each of them, including Judy, in the waiting room outside the intensive care unit. Neither Bill nor Judy had said anything about their imminent break-up to Bill's parents or to Bill's sister, Kristi. Bill acted the concerned and dutiful son, demanding to see the doctor as soon as he arrived at the hospital. Thirty minutes later, the family's physician, Dr. John Cabaniss, met with the Wilson family. He explained they did not yet know how damaging the stroke had been nor what her prospects for recovery would be. For now, Debra was almost completely paralyzed.

Bill's father was devastated. Despite his years, Eric Wilson had always seemed the epitome of robust health and vitality. Almost overnight, he had become old. With his disheveled appearance and his confused and uncertain manner, he presented a pitiful figure. Despite the fact that Bill and his family had shown her so little affection over the years, Judy found her heart reaching out to him.

Eric Wilson spent the rest of that day and most of the next in a state of almost semi-consciousness, waiting for Dr. Cabaniss to meet with them again for an update on Debra. When he did, the prognosis was not good. Debra remained in critical condition and had lapsed into a coma.

"She could come out of it at any time, or she could remain comatose for an indefinite period," he advised them. "There is really no way to tell."

"I want the best specialists for her. I want everything possible to be done!" blustered Bill.

The doctor gave him a weary look. "I assure you, Mr. Wilson, she has the absolute best care. We are monitoring her around the clock. We will let you know immediately of any change."

After the doctor left, the family huddled together to outline a plan of action. They decided that Eric, who wanted to spend every waking moment at his wife's side, would move into a condominium in town rather than make the forty-minute commute to the hospital each day. Three days later, Kristi delivered her father to a leased condominium just a few minutes from the hospital. She had furnished the place tastefully and brought in some of her father's favorite things from his home at Oakleigh—his easy chair, a small desk, and a few paintings. She had also hired a staff of servants and made sure they knew what was expected of them.

During the long afternoons he spent at the hospital and the lonely nights at home alone, Eric had time to think. He contemplated his life, specifically his role at Wilson Industries. He had always been the main force behind it, putting off thinking about who would actually take over if something happened to him. His wife's stroke acted as a wake-up call. He could no longer ignore that he was coming to the end of his business career and had to start turning over some of the operations to Bill. But his son had not shown any real brilliance in his job, other than his knack for getting other people to do his work for him. In fact, Bill had shown less and less interest in managing the affairs of the business. Although Bill had been somewhat helpful in expanding the operation—mainly because he was willing to jet off to anywhere, anytime to complete a deal—Eric had no confidence in Bill's trustworthiness or his ability to lead without relying too much on the capable staff he had assembled. Although Eric wanted Bill to be the one to take things over, the reports he had received of his son's adventures on his "business trips" underscored Eric's misgivings.

Ten days after Debra's stroke, Eric returned to Oakleigh for an afternoon to take care of some business, including a review of his personal papers. While in his study, he received a call from Dr. Cabaniss.

"Mr. Wilson?" came the subdued voice over the phone. "I'm sorry to have to call you with some bad news. Your wife has taken a turn for the worse. Her vital signs are weakening, and there's a chance...well, Mr. Wilson, frankly, I'm afraid she may not last much longer. I suggest you and your family get over here as soon as you can."

Eric phoned both Kristi and Bill, but had to leave messages on their voice mails, as both were out. Then, he hastily replaced the personal papers in the fireproof box where he kept them. In his rush to leave the house, however, he forgot to put the box back into the wall safe, to which only he had the combination.

Fifteen minutes later, Bill arrived at the house to check on his father. He let himself in with his own key and called out but was met by silence. He checked his parents' bedroom and the study, but could see his dad had left, presumably, for the hospital. As he turned to leave the study, he noticed the box on his father's desk.

What's the hurt in just looking, thought Bill to himself.

Quickly, he rummaged through the box, finding several stock certificates, insurance policies, and finally, his father's will. Having never seen it before, Bill scanned the document, looking for his name. According to the terms of the will, Wilson Industries would go to his mother if his father preceded her in death. When they both were gone, the family business would be divided between Bill and Kristi, with the son receiving seventy-five percent of the pie and the daughter the remaining twenty-five percent. To make up the difference, Kristi would receive the stocks, bonds, and mutual funds Eric owned. The two heirs would retain equal rights to Oakleigh.

Then Bill noticed several sheets of notebook paper with the will where Eric had obviously been doing some figuring. Several equations were listed and scratched out, each showing different amounts of the business going to Bill and his sister. The last one, which had not been scratched out, showed a majority of the business going to Kristi.

Bill replaced the documents in the file box and arranged it on the desk just as he had found it. Then he left for the hospital and met with the family in the waiting room outside the intensive care unit. Dr. Cabaniss joined them.

"Well, the good news is that she has stabilized and is resting comfortably. Her situation is not as dire as we first thought."

"Does that mean she's going to recover?" asked Kristi anxiously.

"This type of case is just too difficult to predict. She could remain in her present condition for a day, a week, or even months. We just don't know. Right now, I would say there's no reason for you to stay. We'll notify you if there's any change."

Bill, Kristi, Eric, and Judy left the hospital, promising to phone each other immediately if any of them heard from the hospital.

On his drive back to Oakleigh and the guest house where he now lived, Bill's thoughts drifted to the documents he had discovered in his father's house. His concern had shifted from his mother, who lay in a coma, to his father and the changes the old man could be planning to make—changes that definitely would not be in Bill's best interest. He had to do something before his father made those changes permanent and legal. But what?

September 9, 1978

Three days later, as Bill sat in the guest house kitchen finishing his lunch of a roast beef sandwich and a bottle of beer, the telephone rang.

"Hello, Bill? Bill Wilson?" a voice asked on the other end.

"Yes, this is Bill Wilson," he replied. "Who's this?"

The voice cackled a laugh that ended in a dry cough. "Don't you know who this is, Bill? Come on, I can't believe you've forgotten me."

It took a minute for Bill to recognize the voice. When he did, his blood ran cold.

"Hello, Jack," he finally said. "Where are you?"

"That's better," the voice said. "I knew you couldn't forget an old friend."

"Where are you?" Bill repeated.

"Not far from you."

"You're out?"

"That's right. I was a model prisoner for twelve and a half years, and they figured I had paid my debt. Glad to be breathing the free air again."

Bill closed his eyes leaned against the wall, still recovering from the shock.

"You understand I couldn't contact you while you were doing your time, don't you?" he asked.

"Sure, Bill. I didn't expect you to bring me cookies during visiting hours on Sunday afternoons."

"What is it you want?" he asked.

"You sound a little anxious, old buddy. But let me assure you. There's no need to worry. We made a deal, and we both kept our ends of it. I took the fall, and you paid me. Nobody knows anything, and nobody will ever know any different, at least not from me. A deal is a deal."

Bill's mind raced back to the night nearly thirteen years ago when he and Jack Higgins, an employee at the time at Wilson Industries, were driving back to Plaquemine with a woman who also worked at the mill. They had spent an evening drinking and dancing at a Cajun dance hall near New Orleans. All three had consumed enough alcohol to float a boat, and they had capped off the evening snorting about a quarter ounce of Bill's nose candy. On the way home, they had stopped at a rest area along the highway, where Bill and Jack spent about an hour taking turns with the more-than-willing woman in the picnic area behind the restrooms. He was, at that time, actively living the life that earned him the reputation as a wild and crazy rich kid.

Jack offered to drive home, but Bill shook him off, insisting he was sober enough to drive. Somewhere along that dark highway he found out he wasn't. Driving too fast around a sharp curve, Bill lost control of the car, sending it careening off the road and smack into a utility pole. Bill, who had a seatbelt on, received only cuts and bruises. Jack, sound asleep in the back seat, didn't receive a scratch. But the woman, who had been sitting unbuckled in the passenger seat, shot through the windshield and was killed instantly.

In addition to the criminal charges he knew would be brought against him, Bill was well aware of how the incident would affect his career at Wilson Industries. Thinking quickly, he offered Jack a hundred thousand dollars to confess to being the driver of the car and take responsibility for what had happened. It took Jack only a heartbeat to think about and then accept the deal.

When the police arrived at the scene of the accident, Higgins was arrested and charged with negligent homicide while driving under the influence. In frisking Higgins, the cops also found some of Bill's coke on him, along with a hundred dollars cash, and they added possession and selling of an illegal substance to the charges. Although unaware of Bill's true role in the accident, and his dealing at the scene, Bill's parents had no desire for their name to be tainted by any connection to an accidental loss of life. Thanks to the considerable influence of the Wilson name and a close relationship with the publisher of the local newspaper, the incident received only cursory attention by the media. The family also provided Higgins with an attorney, who plea-bargained the case down to a lesser manslaughter offense and got his client off with a twenty-five-year sentence with eligibility for parole after serving at least half the time.

Now the shadow from the past had reappeared. Bill smelled a shake-down in the making.

"So what can I do for you, Jack?" he asked.

"Bill, I used up all the money you gave me to pay off some loan sharks who were breathing down my neck. I'm sorry to say, all that money is gone." Higgins paused to cough again. "I was your best friend back then, Bill. I did you a big favor. Now I need a favor from you."

"What kind of a favor?" Bill asked warily.

"I need you to give me a job. I want to go straight and clean. That's all I'm asking for. A job so I can make a decent living. Who else could I go to? Where could I find a job around here? I need you to help me out here, Bill. How about it?" Higgins said.

Bill thought for a long moment. Whatever else Jack Higgins was, he was a man of his word. He had proven that with his silence during the investigation and the trial. So if Jack was planning to blackmail him now, he would have come out and asked for money right away. Bill sensed an opportunity. Higgins' resurfacing at this particular time could be the answer he was looking for.

"Jack, we need to get together to talk," he said. "I've got some ideas to run by you, and I don't want to get into them on the phone. Let's have lunch tomorrow. I'll meet you at the diner downtown at noon. You remember Bubba's joint, don't you? Nothing's changed there except the waitresses; they're all fat and ugly!"

Jack laughed. "Sure, I remember Bubba's," he said. "What time?"

"Around one. See you there."

Bill hung up the phone. His mind had shifted into fifth gear, speeding toward a solution to the problem of the revision of his father's will.

Higgins was seated at a corner booth at Bubba's Diner when Bill arrived a few minutes before one the next day. The seedy place had not changed in years, the same mismatched tables and chairs in various stages of decay scattered around the room. A disinterested cook hovered over a grill long overdue for a cleaning, and a tired-looking waitress was writing an order for a trucker sitting at the counter. Bill chose the place knowing that the clientele it attracted would not be the same people he would encounter at his country club, nor would any eyebrows be raised at this meeting between Wilson and a man that even the Plaquemine gossips did not recognize.

Higgins had not changed much either. His short stocky frame appeared fit and well-muscled, which had probably served him well while in prison.

The dark hair he had once worn down to his shoulders was shorter and a little thinner now. A scar running down his left forearm looked relatively new, no doubt the result of an encounter with other inmates in the Louisiana State Correctional Facility, where he had been incarcerated.

Bill walked straight to where Jack was seated and sat down. Jack did not get up.

"Good to see you, Bill," Higgins said, but he did not extend his hand. "Thanks for meeting with me."

"How are you?" Bill asked.

"Okay for a man who just spent over twelve years of his life waking up every morning wondering how he would get through the day. Prison is not a place you want to be, I promise you."

Bill had expected Higgins to play up the tremendous sacrifice he had made for him by taking the fall for the accident. He was not disappointed.

"So what's next?" Bill asked. "You're on parole?"

"Right, I report weekly to my parole officer in Baton Rouge. They say they'll get some employment leads for me, but that's crap. I'm too old to flip burgers or cut grass. I need a job, Bill."

The waitress appeared at their table.

"What can I get you guys?" she asked, looking at Bill.

"I'll have a Bud," Bill said.

"The same," Higgins added.

She turned to leave, then stopped.

"Excuse me, but don't I know you?" she asked Bill.

Oh, God, that's the last thing I want to hear, Bill thought.

"I don't think so," he said, looking away.

"Sure I do!" she exclaimed. "It's been years, but I never forget a face. Especially yours. We went to school together a hundred years ago. You're Bill Wilson—the rich kid. Your daddy owns most of the parish. You dated my friend, Cynthia Lee, remember? Cute little blonde? She's married now with four kids, poor thing. Lives in Baton Rouge. I'm Brenda Reed. You don't remember me?"

Bill looked closely at the woman. She looked to be just a little over five feet tall with streaked blonde hair and roots long overdue for a touch up. The heavy makeup she wore hid a face that as a teenager might have been attractive, but had hardened with age. Twenty years of standing on her feet as a waitress for ten hours a day and smoking a couple of packs of cigarettes while she tried to bum free drinks at the town's bars every night had taken their toll. Bill couldn't place her but vaguely remembered her friend, Cynthia. They had gone out a few times, but Bill had been looking far beyond Plaquemine for his future.

Bill snapped his fingers and flashed his most charming smile. "Of course! Now I remember you," he lied. "Good to see you again. It's been a long time."

"Be right back with your beers," she said, and gave Bill a big smile.

Bill turned to Jack Higgins.

"Jack," he began, "you said you needed money, and it just so happens that I need someone for a job. Maybe we can work out an arrangement."

"Wait a minute," Higgins said. "I said I needed a job, not money. I want some regular work, not a quick fix."

"Hear me out," Bill continued. "I'm not talking about a permanent arrangement, but I am talking about a lot of money. I'll tell you this, though. What I tell you stays at this table. If it doesn't, I can assure you the consequences for you will be very serious. You understand what I'm saying?"

"I'm getting the feeling this is going to be something I might not want to hear," Jack said.

"Then you need to walk away right now," Bill said, "and we'll forget we ever had this conversation. Let me say, though, that the opportunity you're going to have to make a big chunk of money will be the only thing I'm going to offer you. You need to make up your mind right now."

The waitress arrived with the beers, breaking the icy tension of the conversation.

"Here you are, guys," she said, placing the Budweiser longnecks in front of them. "How's everything going with you, Bill? I see you're wearing a wedding ring. Did you marry somebody local?"

"No, my wife comes from Colorado. I've been married now for ten years and have an eight-year-old son."

"She must be a damn good woman for you to stay around that long. If she knew as much about you as I do, she never would have married you!" she said with a wink and a laugh. Then seeing the startled look on Bill's face, she kiddingly slapped his shoulder. "Just givin' you a hard time, Bill."

"Brenda! Stop your flirtin'! Order's up," yelled the cook, and Brenda moved away.

Bill looked back at Jack.

"So what have you decided?" he asked. "Do I continue?"

Jack thought for a second, then gave Bill a cold, steely look.

"Go ahead."

Bill took a long pull on his beer.

"Jack," he began, "I have some very serious problems on my radar screen, and it doesn't appear that they are going to vanish on their own. I need to eliminate them."

"These problems," Higgins said, "I take it they are caused by a certain person."

"That's right."

"And this person needs to be removed from the picture."

"Right again."

Jack drained almost half his beer at one pull.

"Bill, you've known me for a long time, and you know I'm no choir boy. But the stuff I've been into, boosting a few cars here and there, some nickel-and-dime scams, running a little coke and pot out of New Orleans—that's all been minor league action. I'm not a player for having somebody hit. Shit, Bill, I wouldn't know how to begin planning the—"

"That's not a problem," Bill interrupted. "The whole operation will be mapped out for you. You'll just be the person who carries it out."

Jack Higgins fidgeted with his coaster, turning it around and around, his uneasiness palpable.

"I...I don't know, Bill," he stammered. "What if—"

"'What if' is bullshit," Bill cut in. "What if people in hell had ice water? Then it wouldn't be hell, would it? What if you don't find a job? What if your parole officer finds a gun in your car and you get sent back to prison?"

"A gun!" Jack stared at Bill in amazement. "So you're putting the squeeze on here?"

"No, no squeeze, just business," Bill said, matter-of-factly. "Jack, you'll be taking a risk, but I'm prepared to make it worth your while. The job pays two hundred thousand dollars. Now, it seems to me you have three choices. You can walk away right now, in which case there's a good chance your parole officer will become extremely interested in everything you do until he finally finds something to send you back to prison for. Or you can go to the cops with this story, in which case you'll have to convince them to take your word—the word of an ex-con with a record as long as your arm—over the word of a respected businessman and pillar of the community. Or you can choose option number three—do the job and walk away with two hundred grand." Bill lifted the beer bottle to his lips for a quick swig. "The choice is yours."

Sitting back in his chair, Bill watched Jack digest what he had just said.

"I guess I never realized what a son of a bitch you really are," Higgins said.

"And you still don't," Bill snapped. "Now are you in or out?"

Jack looked directly into Bill's eyes. The venom he saw there convinced Jack he was dealing with someone far more ruthless than he had ever dreamed of being himself. He had thought to squeeze Bill slightly for some kind of cushy job where he could hold what he had done for him over his head and coast relatively easily for the rest of his life. Wilson had deftly turned the tables on him. He realized he had little choice in the matter. He would do the job and have a nice chunk of change with which to vanish.

"I'm in," he said, "all the way. Who needs to disappear from your life?"

Bill drained the last of his beer.

"My father," he said without emotion.

"You want to kill your father?" Jack sat back hard in his seat. "What kind of a human being wants to kill his own father? You poor bastard, you must be losing your mind. What a son of a bitch! Your own father! Shit!"

Bill remained expressionless, unfazed by Higgins' shock.

"Tell you what, if everything goes as planned, I'll throw in an extra fifty thousand."

Brenda came back to their table.

"More beer guys?" she asked, picking up their empties.

"No," Bill said getting up to leave. "Just a check."

September 11, 1978

Jack Higgins had always been a light sleeper. The time he spent in prison had exacerbated that condition, and he had grown accustomed to dozing through the night, never really falling into a deep sleep. After his conversation with Bill Wilson, his sleep became even more fitful.

Bill knew he could have hired a professional to do the work for less money than he was paying Jack, but in the back of his mind Bill had a vague outline of a plan that would eventually remove Higgins from the picture after the job was done, thus eliminating any possibility, however remote, of having himself linked to the murder.

Bill had told Higgins he would contact him with further instructions. Two days after their meeting, the phone in Jack's small apartment rang.

"We need to talk," the voice on the other end said.

"Go ahead."

"Not on the phone. Go to the diner and wait by the pay phone. I'll call you there in thirty minutes."

Jack hurried to Bubba's, ordered a beer, then sat at the counter nervously sipping it. Five minutes later the phone rang, and he snatched it on the first ring. Bill instructed Jack to meet him at the north shore of the public fishing lake about twenty minutes outside Plaquemine. Jack lost no time driving there, arriving before Bill. He lit a cigarette and paced as he waited.

A few minutes later Bill drove up in his white Mercedes, parking some distance away from Jack's battered compact car. Jack strode over to Bill's car, opened the passenger door, and quickly slid into the seat.

Bill eyed him closely.

"Jack, you don't look so good," Bill said smoothly. "Everything okay?"

"Hey, I'm here to get instructions on how to kill your dad," Higgins said irritably. "You'll forgive me if I seem a little testy."

"I'm paying you to take care of a problem, not to be testy. If the job is more than you can handle—"

"I can handle it," Jack snapped. "Let's get on with it."

Bill handed Jack two envelopes.

"This one has the money," Bill said. "Seventy-five thousand. You can count it if you like."

Jack took the envelope, opened it, and leafed through the bills.

"Not necessary," he said. "What's the other one?"

"I'll get to that. At our next meeting you will get another fifty thousand dollars—that'll be half up-front, assuming you earn the entire two hundred and fifty. You'll get the last payment when the job is done. This envelope has a map of Oakleigh, a layout of the interior of the home on the grounds where my parents live, and the schedule my father likes to follow. On Saturdays, he always goes to Oakleigh and then the country club. I want you to memorize the map of Oakleigh, then burn the information. I want it to look like a robbery. There's a safe behind my mother's portrait over the fireplace in the den. They keep cash, some jewelry, and other things there. Have him open it before you...before you do the job. My mother is in the hospital, so he'll be the only one in the house. Any questions?"

"Not so far," Jack said. "I'll get back to you if I have any later."

"Wrong," Bill said. "You are never to call me. I'll get in touch with you with the rest of the information and how you're going to handle everything. Understood?"

"Jack looked at Bill sullenly. "Understood."

"Now, get out," ordered Bill. "And don't get in my car again unless I invite you."

As Jack watched Bill drive away, the enormity of what he was about to do began to sink in.

September 15, 1978

The law offices of George Parker were located on the second floor of the only building that could be considered an office tower in Plaquemine, Louisiana, although it stood just six stories tall. The Parkers were another of Plaquemine's old-money families, having provided legal services to residents in the area since George Parker's great-grandfather settled there in the mid-nineteenth century.

Eric Wilson had known George Parker since the two were second graders skipping school to swim and fish in Bayou St. Jacques just a short bike ride from Plaquemine. As Eric grew older and assumed the helm of Wilson Industries, George had followed in the footsteps of his forefathers and entered the practice of law. Eric chose to continue his relationship with his old friend, having Parker's law firm serve as the corporate attorneys handling all the legal work for Wilson Industries. Choosing some high-powered legal beagles in their paneled offices in Baton Rouge over the comfortable familiarity of George Parker had never entered Eric Wilson's mind.

On a warm afternoon two weeks after his wife had been admitted to the hospital, Eric took the elevator up to the offices of George Parker. Normally he would walk up the single flight of stairs, but Eric had been experiencing abdominal problems and some pain in his chest, and his doctor had insisted he slow down. Eric knew his discomfort was due primarily to his distress over his wife's condition and uncertain prognosis. But he couldn't deny another source of his anxiety—the continued irresponsible behavior of his son.

Eric knew Bill's marriage to Judy was falling apart. He imagined the worst case scenario of a vicious court fight over the families assets, most notably Wilson Industries. He felt sure the couple's separation was one of the reasons behind Debra Wilson's stroke. If Judy asked for a divorce, Wilson Industries could be at risk.

Eric had been plagued by troubling questions over a possible divorce. What would Judy ask for in a divorce settlement? Had Bill had the sense to draw up a pre-nuptial agreement, protecting the family business from a go-for-the-throat attorney who smelled the possibility of a huge settlement? Were their problems due to infidelity on Bill's part, which could nullify a pre-nuptial? And how would the breakup affect Bill? Bill's work performance had rapidly deteriorated already, and legal proceedings had not even begun. Once again, Eric feared he would have to clean up after his son's untidy lifestyle. This time he would have to keep Bill's irresponsible actions from devastating the business and the family.

"Hello, Mr. Wilson," chirped the receptionist as Eric entered the foyer of the Parker law offices. "What a pleasant surprise." Then she dropped her voice and asked sympathetically, "How are you doing?"

"Well, I've been better, Tina. How are you?" he said.

"I'm fine, but I was so sorry to hear about Mrs. Wilson. How is she?"

"Still no change, I'm afraid. She's been in a coma for two weeks."

"Oh, that's just awful. How may we help you?"

"Is George in?" Eric asked.

"I'm sure he is for you. Let me ring him."

The receptionist phoned George Parker and told him Eric Wilson had popped in to see him. A minute later, Parker appeared in the doorway.

"Eric, how are you? And how's Debra?"

"Hi, George. I'm okay. No change in Debra, though. Have you got a couple of minutes?"

"Sure. Come on back to my office."

George Parker led Eric Wilson through the lobby and into his office at the end of a long corridor lined with a series of paintings of quiet Louisiana bayou scenes. Parker noticed Wilson moved slowly, like a man in a daze. As they entered Parker's corner office, he offered Wilson a seat in a richly uphol-stered chair near a large picture window looking out onto Plaquemine.

"Can I get you a cup of coffee or a soft drink?" Parker asked.

"No thanks, George. I'm fine."

Parker took a seat opposite Eric, then asked, "Now, what brings you here today?"

"Some serious business, I'm afraid, George. I need to make some changes to my will."

"I understand. Do you have them sketched out?" he asked, pointing to the large manila envelope that Wilson had with him.

"I do," he said, opening the envelope and removing a sheaf of papers. He handed them to George. "The way the will reads now, Debra receives Oakleigh, the trust, and most of my liquid assets so that she's taken care of for as long as she lives if I go before her. If Debra dies before me...." his voice broke and trailed off. Parker rose and hurried to a wet bar, where he poured a glass of water from the pitcher there. He returned and handed it to Wilson.

"I'm sorry," Eric said.

"Eric, it's okay. I understand what you're going through."

"The way I've got it now is that when I'm gone, Bill receives seventy-five percent ownership of Wilson Industries. My daughter, Kristi, gets the other twenty-five percent plus all the stock certificates, bonds, and other investments. It works out to be a fairly equal division of the estate. Bill is also named as the primary person in Wilson Industries."

"That's right," Parker said, as he continued to skim over Eric's written instructions.

"I want to move things around a bit. First, I want Bill's seventy-five percent to go to Kristi. Next, the trusts and stock certificates are to be willed to Kristi's kids so they'll have access and ownership of them when they turn twenty-one. I talked to our accounting firm, and they approved the arrangement.

"Last, the twenty-five percent of Wilson Industries originally deeded to Kristi is to be placed in Michael's name. He's Bill's son and will enter the business as he gets older. I want him and his aunt, Kristi, running the company."

George Parker put down his pen and removed his glasses.

"Eric, you realize you've effectively written Bill out of the will?"

"Almost," Eric said. "I want him guaranteed a job at Wilson Industries for as long as his performance is acceptable to Kristi. That means he'll have to toe the line just like everybody else. And he can live in one of the guest houses at Oakleigh as long as he works for Wilson Industries. If he leaves the company, he leaves the house. I know that might sound tough, but I made a lot of mistakes with Bill. By propping him up over the years, I haven't done him any favors. He should have had to learn to sink or swim just like everybody else. But I felt guilty. When he was growing up, I was never around. Not because I didn't want to be, but because I had to run the business. And as you know, he has had license to be the spoiled rich kid all his life. He's been involved for a long time in running the operation, and while he's not totally useless, he'll never make a good CEO. And certain...events have led me to re-think the situation."

"I understand," Parker said.

"Changing the majority ownership of the company to my daughter may seem risky to you, but she's been working in the business for years, though not to the point that Bill has been involved. She's a quick learner, and I feel she can quickly pick up what she needs to know. We've got some very good mid- and upper-level managers and department heads with whom she works well and who could bring her along. And, to be quite honest with you, I have much more faith in her abilities than in Bill's. I have had for years. It's not just Bill's wild and crazy track record as a good-time playboy. More than anyone, you know how many times I've needed your legal help to bail him out of the jams he's gotten himself into. He's shown some promise at times, but lately I've had a lot of doubts about him. I don't want to see him destroy what the family has taken generations to build."

"That's a major move, Eric," Parker pointed out, "changing Kristi from a position of minority to majority ownership."

"I realize that. I've thought it over carefully and it's how I want to structure it. I wish things could be different, but they're not. Bill is my life's disappointment. I've given him every opportunity, and he has never measured up. The future of the business is at stake, and I can't wait any longer for him to grow up and be the man I'd always hoped he would be. If he applies himself and stays clean, he'll have a good future at Wilson Industries. If not, he's on his own."

"You realize Bill will probably contest the will," Parker said. "It will go to court where he'll try to prove you weren't in your right mind when you made the revisions. He'll also point to his years of service to the company. It could get messy."

"I've anticipated that. Since Debra went into the hospital, my health has taken a turn for the worse as well. I guess it's made me realize my mortality. Yesterday I had a complete physical and mental evaluation done. Everything is documented, and all the files with the test results will be forwarded to you. I hope I'll be around for a long time, but when the time comes, you'll have everything you need to ensure my wishes will be carried out."

"Sounds like you have planned all this very carefully," Parker said. "Rest assured we'll draw up the revised will just the way you've outlined it."

"Thank you, George. I knew I could count on you."

Eric Wilson rose to leave and shook his friend's hand.

"Know that our thoughts and prayers are with you and Debra at this difficult time. And please contact me if I can be of further service. We'll take care of this matter immediately and phone you as soon as the new will is ready for your signature."

Parker walked Eric to the office foyer and into the hallway where he pressed the down button for the elevator.

"Think I'll take the stairs instead," Eric said.

"Take care, Eric" Parker said. "I'll be in touch." Eric Wilson noticed the concerned look on George Parker's face, the genuine feeling in his words. As he shuffled down the stairs and out into the street, Eric did not notice a familiar Mercedes parked down the street.

Bill Wilson had been keeping tabs on his father since stumbling across the will on Eric's desk. Watching the old man leave his lawyer's offices confirmed Bill's suspicions, convincing him he had to act quickly if he didn't want to be written out of Wilson Industries.

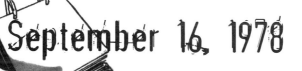

September 16, 1978

Bill had arranged to visit his son the next afternoon at Judy's house on the Oakleigh grounds. Judy and Mike sat on the porch and watched as Bill unloaded several gifts from the car's trunk. As Bill showed Mike the wonders of each present, the phone rang. Reluctantly, Judy went inside to answer it but returned quickly.

"Bill," she said, "the phone's for you."

Bill gave an annoyed sigh, then brushed by Judy and went into the kitchen. "Hello," he said.

"Hey, man, this is Higgins! Remember?"

Bill quickly looked outside to make sure that Judy was out of earshot.

"I told you never to call me!" Bill seethed under his breath. "This is my wife's number!"

"So what? I got tired of waiting for you. I'm ready to get this job done. You hired me to k—"

"Shut up!" Bill interrupted. "Meet me at eleven tonight at the lake and make sure no one sees you." He quietly replaced the receiver and went outside, all smiles.

"Who was that?" asked Judy.

"Just a guy who might do some repairs over at the guest house for me."

"But why wouldn't you use Randy?" Judy asked, referring to the resident handyman at Oakleigh.

Bill turned on her angrily. "What's it to you? It's none of your business, so just stay out of it!"

Judy could see Mike standing behind Bill, a fearful look in his eyes. Not wanting to spoil her son's time with his dad, Judy forced herself to be apologetic.

"You're right. I'm sorry." She smiled reassuringly at Mike. "Why don't I go get us all some lemonade and cookies?"

The rest of Bill's visit passed peaceably. Around six, he returned home to the guest house near his parents' house in which he had taken up residence, fixed a frozen dinner, and watched TV until time to leave to meet Jack Higgins.

Jack had left his apartment and driven around town for almost half an hour before heading to the lake, making sure he wasn't followed. Very little traffic moved around Plaquemine at that hour of the night; it would have been difficult for anyone to tail Jack without being noticed. By the time he drove down the unpaved road that led to the lake, Jack felt confident no one had followed him. He got out, lit a cigarette, and leaned against the car to wait for Bill. The few minutes that passed seemed like hours to Jack. He wondered whether Bill had had second thoughts about having his father killed.

Ten minutes after eleven, Jack saw the headlights of the Mercedes turn onto the lake road. Bill chose to park his car on the other side of the parking lot, a good forty feet away from Jack's car.

"You're late," Jack snapped, as Bill walked toward him.

"Wanted to make sure I wasn't followed," he replied easily. Jack noticed Bill had a small package and an envelope in his left hand.

"Here's the next installment—fifty grand," he said. "Count it if you want."

Jack shook his head.

"Just get on with it."

"Here's what I want you to do. Tomorrow I'm flying to England on business, which my father knows about. He has been staying at a condominium in town to be close to the hospital, but on Saturday nights he goes back to Oakleigh. He and my mother always ate dinner at the Iberville Country Club on Saturday evenings, and he still does. Then he goes home. The staff is off on Saturday night, so no one else will be at the house.

"Steal a set of plates for your car, then drive out to Oakleigh around nine o'clock. Park just past the main entrance to the house. That's important, because I don't want him to be able to see your car. Ring the doorbell. When he comes to the door, tell him you're delivering a registered package addressed to him from England. He'll think it's something from me and open the door. When you hand him the package, shove him inside. Take him to the den, have him open the safe, then do the job. He doesn't keep much cash there, but he'll have some jewelry and some papers. Take whatever's there; I'll get it back from you when we settle up. And don't bother trying to pull a fast one on me. I know what's in the safe. In fact, he'll probably have a gun there, too, so keep your eyes open. Toss the house pretty well, so it looks like the intruder was looking for money and other valuables.

"Afterwards, drive to the Baton Rouge airport and put the car in the long-term parking. Don't forget to get rid of those stolen plates before you park it. Then, take the shuttle to the Holiday Inn. I've already booked a reservation there in the name of Warren Edwards. Check in under that name and pay cash. If they give you a hard time, tell them your wallet and credit cards were stolen. Make sure you have enough money in your suitcase for at least four nights' stay."

Bill then handed him the brown envelope. Jack opened it and found a .38 Colt revolver with a six-inch barrel.

"The numbers have been filed off, and so the piece can't be traced," he said. "On your way to Baton Rouge, throw it off the St. Bernard Parish Bridge as you drive over it. Don't stop. Just open your window, toss it, and keep going."

Higgins looked at the revolver again, somewhat reluctantly. Bill noticed the anxiety in the man's face.

"What's the matter, Jack?" he asked quietly.

"Nothing."

"You're not going soft on me, are you?"

"No. I'm ready. I won't see you again until Baton Rouge, right?"

"You'll hear from me there. I'll contact you about where to meet me and get the rest of your money. Now go on back to town."

Higgins got into his car and left. Bill watched the taillights fade away before he started his Mercedes. He thought about Higgins as he drove home. The man was nervous, too nervous, and Jack wondered whether he had made a mistake in choosing him to do the job. Still, he felt fairly sure Jack's greed and desperation would win out over his fear.

Back home, Bill fixed himself a drink and packed his suitcase for his trip to England. All he had to do now was make sure he got on the plane to England tomorrow and then wait for the phone call from his family with word about the tragic death of his father.

September 18, 1978

On what would be the last evening of his life, Eric Wilson awakened from his nap around five. He dressed in a sports jacket, slacks, and tie, and drove to the Iberville Country Club. Never one to be seen casually attired, he took special care about his appearance at the club, even on the evenings when a coat and tie were not required. He ordered a dinner of roast prime rib of beef, which, he decided during his drive home, had been overcooked. When he arrived back at Oakleigh, he parked and walked slowly through the brightly lit pathway into the house. He checked the answering machine for any phone messages from the hospital concerning his wife's condition, but no message light blinked. He then changed into his pajamas and bathrobe and went into the den to watch television for a while before retiring for the evening.

Eric had no idea he'd been followed home from the club by Jack. Parking some distance from the house, Jack found a spot on the grounds where he could observe the older man's movements, waiting for the right opportunity to strike. About nine-thirty, he returned to his car, started it up, drove it to the spot where Bill had said to park, leaving the engine running. With the package under his left arm, he walked through the pathway to the front door of the Wilson's home. He rang the bell and knocked loudly, then took a deep breath. It didn't calm his pounding heart.

At first, Eric waited for his butler to answer the door. Then, remembering the staff had the evening off, he got up himself and walked through the massive foyer. Who would be knocking on my door at this time of night, he wondered a bit anxiously.

"Who is it?" he asked through the door.

"Mr. Eric Wilson?" Jack asked.

"That's right."

"Sir, I'm with Plaquemine Taxicab. We've been asked to deliver this package to you from England. I need your signature, please." Jack said.

"Oh, that must be from my son, Bill," Eric said. "Just a moment." Eric moved to a panel behind a curtain where he turned the alarm system off, then returned and unlocked the front door.

Jack's heart raced. The moment it took for the door to swing open seemed to last an eternity. He handed Eric a box wrapped in brown paper and bound with string. Before Eric had a chance to turn over the package and read the address, Jack shoved him back inside the house and closed the door. Quickly, he pulled out the revolver from his jacket and shoved it in Eric's face.

"Let's go into your den and open the safe," Jack Higgins ordered.

"There's no safe in this house," Eric said, moving away from Higgins. "Take what you want from my wallet and just go."

Higgins shoved Eric against the wall and jammed the pistol against his throat.

"I'm not going to tell you again," he seethed. The butterflies in Jack's stomach had vanished as soon as the action had begun. His blood now ran ice cold, his focus solely and completely on his mission.

Shocked and frightened, Eric stared into his assailant's eyes. What he saw there, a raw and predatory animal instinct, convinced him to comply with the man's orders. Putting his hands in the air, he didn't struggle as Higgins turned him around and jabbed the pistol into his spine. Slowly they walked to the den. Higgins shoved him towards the fireplace.

"Who are you?" Eric asked. "How do you know where things are in this house? Look, if someone is paying you to do this, I'll pay you to—"

"Shut up!" Higgins spat. "Move the picture and open the safe."

"You *are* being put up to this. How else could you know about the safe?"

Higgins pushed the Colt harder into the old man's back.

"I said 'open it,'" he ordered.

Eric pulled the left side of the painting away from the wall, revealing a recessed safe. He worked the combination until the door opened, then started to reach into the safe.

"That's far enough," Higgins said, remembering that Bill had told him a gun was kept there. "Go over to that chair and sit down."

"Look, whoever you are, just take what you want and—"

"Do it!" Higgins shouted. "Sit down on that chair! Now!"

The old man moved away from the fireplace and fell heavily into the chair next to the sofa, his frightened eyes fixed on Jack. Hesitating for but a moment, Higgins moved behind him and pointed the gun at the back of Eric's head.

"I hate to do this to you, Mr. Wilson, but your no-good son, Bill, has paid me a lot of money to kill you!"

As Jack finished saying the words "kill you," he pulled the trigger and fired. The old man pitched forward and collapsed on the floor, his body quivering slightly. Higgins fired again, and the body lay motionless. A dark pool of blood quickly collected under his head and spread over the antique Oriental rug.

At the sight of blood, Higgins suddenly experienced his first pang of panic. Steady, he told himself, and once again tried to calm himself by taking a deep breath.

Jack went to the window to see if the noise had attracted any attention. He saw nothing. Oakleigh sat a good mile away from the main highway that led to Plaquemine. The closest building to the main house was the guest house in which Bill had taken up residence. The household staff would be gone until Sunday afternoon. The house Judy and Bill had shared was well over two miles away on the other side of the plantation grounds. Everything was going as Bill said it would.

Jack put the pistol back into the pocket of his jacket, then crossed the room to the safe where he removed a packet of cash, several sealed envelopes, and a .32 caliber Taurus handgun. He placed all the items in a black satchel he had been carrying and then returned to where the old man lay on the floor. He felt for a pulse on the carotid artery but found none.

Higgins spent an anxious few minutes strewing everything around the den and Eric Wilson's office to make the house look as if it had been ransacked, then raced upstairs to do the same with the main bedroom. Returning downstairs, he paused to pick up the delivery package from the foyer. He decided to leave the television on and the door to the safe open. After taking one last look around the den, he hurried out, closing the door to the house softly behind him. He strode to his still idling car and quickly drove away.

Once on the highway, certain that no one had seen him, Jack began to relax. He was surprised at how calm he had remained during the whole incident, considering he had never imagined himself a professional hitman, capable of doing what he had just done. Even during his incarceration, when he'd suffered attacks from other inmates, he had been hesitant to use the

homemade knife he had fashioned in the prison metal shop to protect himself. But now the die was cast.

As he drove across the St. Bernard Parish Bridge, he smiled grimly to
himself at the symbolism. He had crossed a bridge tonight. No longer was he
some small-time hood. He had moved into big-time crime. Instead of regret-
ting having taken a life, he felt a sense of pride for having the guts to go through
with it. Rolling down his window, he tossed the revolver out and across the
narrow lane of the bridge. It sailed over the railing and disappeared.

As he exited the freeway in Baton Rouge, he noticed the gloves he still
wore, which had kept the gun powder residue from clinging to his hands.
Removing them, he found a dumpster behind a restaurant and shoved them
under a pile of potato peelings. Before heading to the Holiday Inn, he
found a dark street where he removed the license plates, which he buried in
a nearby field.

No way they can trace any of this to me now, he thought. After stopping
at an all-night liquor store for a bottle of rye, he made his way to the hotel.

✳   ✳   ✳

The next afternoon, just after three London time, the telephone rang in
Bill Wilson's room at the Trafalgar Hotel just off Trafalgar Square. Bill let it
ring three times before answering it.

"Bill, this is Steve," the voice on the other end said.

"Steve, hi," said Bill, then he paused for effect. "Oh, God, has something happened with Mom? Is she…is she better? She's not…." Bill let his
voice trail away as though he couldn't bring himself to say the words.

"No, Bill, I'm…I'm not calling about Debra. There's been no change in
her condition." Bill heard what sounded like a sob come across the line. "But,
I do have some terrible news. I just…I hate like hell to have to tell you this on
the phone."

"Steve, what is it? What's wrong?" Bill asked, feigning anxiety.

"Bill, it's your father. He's been…murdered. It happened last night. Looks
like someone robbed him at home and then killed him."

Bill remained silent for a moment.

"Are you there?" Steve asked.

"Yes," Bill said quietly. "I'm here. I just…I'm just stunned. I can't
believe it." Again he paused, as though he were quietly mourning the passing

of his father. "I'll try to get back home as soon as I can. Unfortunately, I've probably missed the last flights today for the States. Most of them leave in the morning or early afternoon." He hesitated again, hoping his brother-in-law would assume he was in shock. "I'll phone now to book a flight for tomorrow morning and see you as soon as I get home."

"Bill, you won't be able to get into Oakleigh. The police have taken over the house. They have their forensic people there checking for fingerprints and whatever else they need to do. You'd better come to our house."

"Oh, God, how's Kristi?" Bill asked.

"Just how you'd expect her to be. Completely broken up. The doctor's here now giving her a sedative," Steve said.

"Tell her I'll be on the next flight home. And, Steve…well, thanks."

Bill hung up the phone and walked to the window. Crowds of tourists oozed through Trafalgar Square, but Bill didn't see them. His mind was racing, trying to analyze how successfully Higgins had been in completing the job.

When Bill arrived into the Baton Rouge Airport late the next afternoon, he found a pay phone and dialed the number for Kristi's home. His brother-in-law answered.

"Steve, this is Bill. I just landed at the airport and will be at the house in about a half hour. How's Kristi doing?"

"Well, she's a little better. Judy's with her."

"Judy?"

"Yeah, she's been with Kristi since we heard about the…about Eric. She's been a big help."

"Do the police know anything yet?" Bill asked.

"Nothing. They're still investigating."

"I'll see you in a while," Bill said and hung up the phone, his spirits buoyed by the news that the police hadn't any leads in the murder as yet.

Driving up to his sister's house, Bill wasn't prepared for what he saw. Several cars lined the suburban street, and dozens of people stood out in the yard talking. As he walked up the stairs to the porch, people called out his name, offering their sympathy and offering to help in any way.

Kristi came rushing out the front door and flung herself into his arms crying uncontrollably. Seeing his sister's grief, Bill actually felt tears in his eyes.

"Bill, how could this happen? I can't believe Dad is dead!" she cried. "He was so good to everyone. Why would someone murder him? And

Mom....." Kristi let a sob escape. "Poor Mom, in the hospital. Can you imagine telling her? When she finds out, this will just kill her, too! Oh, God, why did this happen?"

"Some things we're just not meant to understand," Bill said. "We've still got each other. We'll get through this together."

Steve came onto the porch and embraced his brother-in-law, followed by Judy, who gave him a warm hug as well.

"Bill, I'm so sorry about your dad. He was a fine man. It's just terrible that he had to suffer through that."

Bill looked at her coldly, surprised to see she had been crying. She looked truly upset over the death of a man who had never accepted her as a member of the family nor shown her any genuine warmth as a father-in-law.

"Hello, Judy. How have you been?" he said flatly. Not bothering to wait for a reply, he nodded toward Kristi, who continued to sob quietly, and said, "Why don't you take her somewhere away from all these people."

"Come on, Kristi, let's go upstairs for a while," said Judy, gently steering Kristi through the front door.

Bill turned back to Steve.

"Who in the Plaquemine Police Department is handling the case?" Bill asked.

"An investigator named Lieutenant Lucas," Steve answered. "He and his partner questioned all of us and the staff yesterday afternoon. The cook found your dad yesterday morning when she came to get lunch started. She phoned us at home crying hysterically, and we called the police right away."

"Has anything been done about funeral arrangements?" Bill asked.

"No, not yet."

"I'll contact Marceau's tomorrow," Bill said. "If Kristi feels up to it, we'll go down there together. If not, I'll meet with them."

"That reminds me, I've got some calls to make," said Steve. "I'll see you a little later."

As Steve went back inside, Judy came out on the porch. She walked over to Bill and put a hand on his arm.

"Are you okay?" she asked.

"What do you care?" he asked bitterly.

"Bill, your father has been murdered. The family is torn apart. Can't you be just a little civil at a time like this? You haven't even asked how your son is."

"I'm sure you've done your best to convince him I'm a monster. I hear you've got an attorney. Go ahead. Do your worst. We'll see who comes out ahead."

Judy shook her head. "Nobody wins in a situation like this. You know that. And I haven't said anything bad about you to Mike. I don't have to. You've already done a pretty good job of showing him what kind of person you are all by yourself."

She turned to go back into the house. A few minutes later, she emerged with Michael. He looked at his father with large, scared eyes but clung to Judy.

Bill knelt down so he looked eye to eye with his son.

"Hi, Mike," Bill said. "How you doin', buddy? You okay?"

"I guess so," the youngster said, still clinging to his mother. He made no effort to go to his father.

"Why don't you go on home with your mother," Bill said. "I'll be by to see you as soon as I get finished making some phone calls."

"If you need help with any of the arrangements, just let me know," Judy said to Bill as she walked Michael to her car. As they drove away, Bill could see the little boy's expressionless face staring out the window at him.

Bill finally went into his sister's house, where he chatted with well-wishers for the rest of the afternoon. It was after six when Steve came up to him and put a friendly hand on his shoulder.

"Bill, why don't you go home? I know you must be worn out."

"I am pretty tired," Bill admitted. "By my watch, it's about eight hours later than here."

Kristi, who had come downstairs a few minutes earlier, handed Bill a grocery bag. "Here, take this with you. There's enough food in there for a couple of days. People have been bringing stuff by for the last two days so we wouldn't have to worry about cooking," she said. "Call me tomorrow, and I'll go with you to Marceau's Funeral Home."

"You don't have to," Bill said. "I can do it if you're not up to it."

"No," she said. "I need to go."

"Okay, I'll call you around nine."

Kristi walked with Bill to his car and gave him a last, heartfelt squeeze.

When Bill arrived home, instead of going inside, he sat in the swing on the porch and thought about his next move. He felt sure his father hadn't had time to sign a revised will, meaning that Bill was still in line to inherit the lion's share of Wilson Industries. Judy, he knew, would proceed with her plans for a divorce. However, he believed he had enough pull with the right people to drag that out long enough for her to run out of money for attorney's fees and, hopefully, give up. They could live separate lives and he would be essentially free to do what he wanted. Tomorrow he would phone "Warren Edwards" in Baton Rouge to schedule a meeting with him. That would wrap up the last loose end in his scheme.

hree days after his death, Eric Wilson was laid to eternal rest at Forest Lawn Cemetery just outside Plaquemine. Most of Iberville Parish turned out for the funeral. It rivaled the send-offs given in the past to some of Louisiana's most prominent political leaders. The local newspaper ran a front-page story about a man the whole town loved and respected. Following the funeral, almost two hundred friends, family members, and employees of Wilson Industries went to Kristi's house. The Oakleigh staff, themselves broken up over the loss of Eric Wilson, had prepared a huge buffet. Two of Plaquemine's residents were not in attendance: Debra Wilson, who remained in a coma at the hospital, and Jack Higgins, who still anxiously awaited a phone call in his hotel room in Baton Rouge.

Among the last of the guests to leave the post-funeral meal was Lieutenant Frank Lucas of the Plaquemine Police Department. He stopped to speak to Bill Wilson, who was shaking hands with the departing guests.

"I'm sorry about the loss of your father, Mr. Wilson," Lucas said. "He was a great leader in this community."

Bill eyed him coldly. "I wish you had some news to tell me about finding the person responsible for his murder."

"We still don't have much to go on," Lucas said, "but we are working on some theories."

"Like what, for instance?"

"Well, since there was no forced entry into the house, we feel your father probably knew his assailant. It appears he let whoever it was into the house himself. And your father's body showed no marks of being beaten before he was killed. This leads us to believe the killer didn't have to pry the information about the wall safe out of your father. Somehow, the killer already knew where the valuables were kept. The killer showed up late Saturday night, your father let him in without incident, and he—or she, I suppose—shot him." The lieutenant pulled a small notebook out of his suit coat pocket. "It doesn't have the makings of a professional hit, though."

"Why do you say that?" Bill asked.

Lucas flipped through his notes. "Well, for one thing, your father was shot twice. The gun used in the killing was a .38 caliber. The trajectory of the bullet indicates that he was shot once at close range from the left rear side of his head. The other shot came from a little farther away. A professional would have probably used a different caliber gun, and he wouldn't have needed a second shot."

Bill felt his pulse quicken slightly.

"Does that mean you suspect someone the family knew? One of the servants maybe?"

"Right now, everyone is a suspect, Mr. Wilson. We questioned the entire staff, your sister, her husband, and your wife. We also talked to your plant manager, David Oliver. We'll keep digging, and I feel confident we'll bring whoever did it to justice."

"I hope it's sooner rather than later," Bill said.

Lucas looked at Bill, his gaze steady and without warmth. "Yeah, me, too. By the way, Mr. Wilson, do you travel often to Europe on business?"

Bill felt his heart kick into gear again.

"No, not that often," he said. "Usually about once a year. With our expansion into foreign markets, I'll probably be going more often now. Why do you ask?"

"Just curious," Lucas answered. "We'll be in touch."

Bill watched the lieutenant walk to his car, staying on the porch until Lucas drove away.

Why would he ask about my going to Europe, Bill wondered. Was he thinking that I had manufactured an alibi by being out of the country? Bill smiled smugly to himself. The lieutenant wouldn't get anywhere if he followed that line.

After saying goodbye to Kristi and Steve, Bill got into his Mercedes and headed home. Halfway there, however, he pulled into a gas station, where he parked next to the pay phone. He didn't pick up the receiver immediately, but first flipped impatiently through the yellow pages. Then, finding the number he needed, Bill deposited a dime and dialed.

"Holiday Inn. How may I help you?"

"Warren Edwards' room, please."

The phone rang just once.

"Hello?" came Jack's anxious voice over the wire.

"It's me,"

"Shit, it's about time you called," Higgins said, fear and anger mingled in his voice. "What took you so long?"

"Been pretty busy, Jack. Arrangements to be made, people to visit, a funeral to go to—you know, the whole routine."

"I need the rest of my money. I want to leave Baton Rouge."

"I think that would be a good idea. Meet me tonight at the same spot at the lake around midnight."

"I'll be there."

Bill continued his drive home to the guest house that sat just a short distance from the main house at Oakleigh. The barriers and bright yellow police tape were gone. He paused for a moment near the part of the driveway closest to his father's house, then continued on to the cottage. Once inside, he walked into the den and poured himself a Scotch.

Bill took his Scotch out onto the porch. A full moon shone through the thriving oak trees, which formed a canopy over the road from Oakleigh to the main highway. Bill leaned against one of the four columns in front of the guest house, enjoying the surprisingly balmy night. He reflected on how much he had changed from the kid who had grown up in the majestic house just a stone's throw from where he now stood.

And then, vague shadows of doubt crept into his mind over what he had done. Bill tried to dismiss them, telling himself he had taken the right— no, the necessary preemptive action. With his plan to write Bill out of the picture at Wilson Industries, Eric Wilson had forced his son's hand. After all, Bill thought self-righteously, he had spent years working in the family business, grooming himself for the day when he would assume the helm of the empire and steer it to even greater heights than his father and grandfather had ever dreamed of. Why should he sit idly by and watch his father, obviously under severe strain and not thinking clearly since his wife's illness, give away what was rightly his inheritance? No, he banished any second thoughts he might have. He had done what had to be done.

For as long as he could remember, the relationship between Bill and his father had been more of a business arrangement. No deep bond, no abiding love had ever grown between father and son. Ordering his father's murder had not been a move he'd made lightly, but neither would it haunt him.

Driving to the lake later that evening, Bill's thoughts focused only on what he still had to do. In a couple of hours, he could close the chapter on this entire mess. Then he could concentrate on stabilizing his hold on the family business.

September 22, 1978

Bill Wilson found his way to the lake a little after midnight, his headlights cutting through a light fog that had settled in. As he pulled into the parking lot, he saw Higgins leaning against the passenger door of his Dodge, waiting. As he climbed out of the car, Bill did not remove his leather driving gloves as he usually did.

"I'm glad to see you," Jack said nervously. "I want to finalize everything and leave town. The sooner the better."

"Did you bring the things you removed from the safe?" Bill asked.

Jack reached inside the front seat of the car and retrieved the black leather satchel, which held all of the safe's contents. He handed it to Bill, who opened it and rummaged through the contents.

"It's all there," Jack said. "The piece too. You were right. He had a .32 stashed in there with the rest of the things. Now how about my money?"

"Jack, it looks like you did a good job. I've spoken with the cops several times, and they don't appear to have any leads. At least, if they do, they're not talking about them. You followed my directions, and now all my problems have been solved. Except for one."

"What do you mean?" Higgins asked. "I did everything just the way you said. I've even been sitting at the hotel in Baton Rouge going nuts waiting for you to call. What else is there?"

Bill tossed the black satchel into the passenger seat of his Mercedes. When he turned back around to face Higgins again, he was holding a 9mm Beretta. The blood drained from Jack's face.

"Jack, I'm sorry about this, but I can't afford to leave any loose ends. You are the only person who can tie me to the murder."

"You son of a bitch. I didn't expect this from you! I trusted you to keep your end of the bargain."

"We all make mistakes, Jack. Sorry about this. Now turn around and start walking toward the fishing pier."

"Bullshit! You want to kill me? You'll have to look me in the eye to do it. You got the stomach for that, rich boy?"

Bill looked directly into Higgins' eyes and pulled the trigger. Surprised, Jack gave a grunt and clutched his chest. As he fell slowly to the ground, he rasped, "I hope you pay for this, you bastard."

Bill kneeled down to feel for a pulse, which he found still beating faintly. He fired one more shot into Jack's left temple.

Jack was a tough bastard, I'll give him that, Bill thought. He looked out into the darkness that enveloped the lake. He could not hear a sound, not even a cricket. The fog had cloaked the area like a blanket.

Bill hurriedly rummaged through Jack's pockets. He found a wallet and a set of car keys, along with the receipt for his room at the Holiday Inn in Baton Rouge. Bill placed them all in the black satchel. Next he made a thorough search of the car, finding only Jack's suitcase. Forcing it open, Bill looked through the case, finding nothing but clothes. No papers, no evidence, nothing Jack had packed could link Bill to him. Bill put the suitcase in the trunk of the Mercedes. Tomorrow he would put it in the giant waste bin at Wilson Industries, where it would be smashed, compacted, and sent off to the dump. He would dispose of his gun the same way he'd instructed Jack to get rid of his. The police would never find it.

Bill surveyed the scene once more, looking for anything that might give him away. Satisfied with his work, he got into his car and calmly drove away.

✳ ✳ ✳

Lieutenant Lucas arrived early at the station house the next morning, hoping to get a head start on his day. He had just sat down at his desk with a cup of black coffee when the phone buzzed.

"Yeah?" he said, pushing down the intercom button.

"Call on line two. Guy says he's got a dead body on his hands."

Lucas sighed. "So much for catching up on the paperwork," he muttered, as he punched up line two.

The caller was short and to the point. He'd gone out before daybreak to go fishing at the lake. When he drove into the parking lot, he'd seen a car but hadn't pay much attention to it. When he came back in around seven-thirty, however, he'd noticed a man lying next to it, dried blood crusted on his head and chest.

Lucas sent a deputy out to interview the man. When Lucas's partner, Detective Jerry Simmons, came in about twenty minutes later, they drove out to the scene. They found the sheriff's deputy from Iberville Parish talking with the witness, while a lab tech went over the crime scene.

After hearing the fisherman's story, Lucas asked the deputy to walk a ways with him.

"You got anything else, other than his story?" he asked, as they strolled toward the car.

"Yeah, I checked out the vehicle identification number. The car was registered to—" he consulted his notebook "—a Jack Higgins, no known address. He bought it from Tyler's Used Cars and Rentals in Little Rock."

Lucas wrote down the info in his own pocket notebook.

"That's pretty quick work, Dixon," he said to the deputy, then added with a wry smile, "I'd better watch out, or before I know it, you'll have my job."

The deputy grinned back. "I think you're safe, sir—at least for the time being."

When they returned to headquarters, Lucas called the owner of the car lot.

"Yeah, I remember him," said Fred Tyler when questioned about the sale. "Jack used to live in Little Rock. I knew him slightly. He did some auto detailing for me, off and on."

"Did you know he'd been in prison?" asked Lucas.

"Well, yeah, but he said he'd been set up. Didn't matter. He did a good job for me—when he showed up."

"How much was the car?" asked Lucas.

"Eighteen hundred. He came in one day, pointed it out, and paid cash."

Lucas paused. "You didn't think that was odd? Him having so much cash?"

"That's not all that strange with my business," Tyler said. "A lot of people come up with the cash to buy my cars. Most of my cars are older models with a lot of mileage since they used to be rentals. I can't charge much for them. Besides, I knew Jack liked the track, so I just figured he'd got lucky and picked a winner."

Lucas thanked Tyler for his cooperation and hung up. Turning to his partner, he told him what he'd found out from Tyler.

"It's kind of strange," Lucas said. "We've got two homicides in Plaquemine, a small, quiet Louisiana town that rarely gets any headlines." He looked at Simmons. "Do you think there's a link?"

Simmons shook his head doubtfully. "They weren't shot with the same caliber gun. And we don't have anything to connect Jack Higgins with Eric Wilson, other than he worked for Wilson Industries a decade ago."

His phone buzzed. "Kristi Walker, line four," the voice on the intercom informed him.

"Any luck yet, Mr. Lucas, on my father's murder?" she asked.

"Sorry, Mrs. Walker, nothing yet. We're still following a few leads."

"I'm wondering…well, I was wondering if a reward might help, you know, get someone to come forward who knows something," Kristi said, somewhat hesitantly. "I spoke with David Oliver, our general manager at Wilson Industries, and he thought it would be a good idea. But Bill—my brother—he thought it might not be appropriate right now." Lucas could hear the agony in her voice. "What do you think? Would it help at all?"

"I think offering a reward would be an excellent idea. It just might flush something out that we might otherwise not find. Under Louisiana law, we're authorized to offer up to ten thousand dollars for information leading to the arrest and conviction of the party or parties responsible. I've already started the paperwork on that."

"I'll have David begin the work from our end as well," Kristi said. "We'll be offering one hundred thousand dollars."

Lucas whistled. "That kind of money makes people a little more inclined to get involved." He was about to hang up, when a thought popped into his head. "By the way, Mrs. Walker, has your father's will been read to the family yet?"

"Not yet. His attorney is out of town on business and won't be back until next week. That's the first thing we'll be doing when he returns."

"Please let me know when you've done that. It just might shed some light on the situation."

September 26, 1978

Brenda Reed followed a familiar routine every Sunday morning, her only day off. After standing on her feet for ten hours a day, six days a week, she usually spent Saturday night making the rounds of the taverns and dance halls in Plaquemine, drinking and partying till all hours. Sundays she indulged herself, lounging in bed until at least ten, then walking down to the corner bakery to buy a gourmet coffee and giant cinnamon roll and carrying them back home to enjoy on her front porch as she read the *Plaquemine Herald*. This particular Sunday, an article in the metro section caught her attention.

The story told of an unsolved homicide at the lake, an event that wouldn't have caused Brenda to think twice, except for the accompanying photo of the victim. With a memory for faces that comes from years in the bar and restaurant trade, Brenda recognized the victim as the man who had been in the diner just a couple of weeks earlier. The story said police had identified the man, but were looking for information as to who had killed him. After a few minutes of indecision, she picked up the phone and called the police station.

"I'm calling about the murder case, the one out at the lake," she told the dispatcher.

She gave her name and number and was told she'd be called by a Lieutenant Lucas. Ten minutes later, her phone rang.

"This is Lieutenant Lucas calling for Brenda Reed."

"This is Brenda Reed," she answered, a knot forming in her stomach. She wondered whether she was doing the right thing.

"Ms. Reed, I was told you might be able to help us in an investigation."

Brenda swallowed hard.

"I…I think I may have some information…about the murder of that man, the one you found dead at the lake."

"Where are you, Ms. Reed? I'd like to come right over."

Brenda hesitated, then said, "I live at Sunrise Village Apartments, 2428 Holly Court, apartment two-twenty-eight."

Lucas hurriedly called Simmons and arranged to pick him up. In less than thirty minutes, the two stood on Brenda Reed's doorstep. She answered the door at the first knock.

"Ms. Reed?" Lucas asked, flashing his badge.

"Yes."

"I'm Lieutenant Lucas, and this is Detective Simmons. May we come in?"

She stepped aside and waved them into the tiny living room.

"Would you like coffee or tea or something?" Brenda asked nervously.

"Thank you, no," Lucas said. "You said you had some information on the Higgins murder case?"

"Please, sit down." Brenda motioned to the slip-covered sofa. "I read there was a reward offered for information on the Wilson murder. Is there anything offered in this case?"

"Not right now. But there may be a reward offered by the state later on if our investigation doesn't turn up anything. What do you have?"

"I was hoping that there would be something in it for me," Brenda said stubbornly.

"Ms. Reed, there may or may not be any reward for information on the Higgins case. But I can assure you that if you are withholding any information on either case, you could be in a lot of trouble. Now, why don't you just tell me what you know, and I can tell you if it might be of value to us."

Brenda said nothing. Instead she arose and moved over to a bureau, where she opened a drawer, poked around, and finally found a pack of Marlboros. She pulled out a cigarette, lit it, and took one long drag. As she exhaled, she turned to face the two men.

"This Higgins, he came into the diner not long ago," she said. "I'd never seen him in there before. He had a couple of beers with another guy. Now he turns up dead. I just…well, it seemed a little strange to me, that's all."

"Who was the man he had the beers with?" Simmons asked.

"Him I know," Brenda said. "Bill Wilson, one of *the* Wilsons of Iberville Parish."

Lucas felt his heart suddenly begin thudding in his chest.

"Ms. Reed," he said slowly, "are you sure?"

"Sure I'm sure," she replied, a bit churlishly, "I went to school with him. He dated my best friend. I ought to know him."

Lucas locked eyes with Simmons, one thought in both their minds.

"Anything else?" Lucas asked.

Brenda shrugged. "That's it. They talked for a while, Wilson paid for their beers, gave me a ten dollar tip, and they left."

Lucas took a card out of his wallet and handed it to Brenda.

"If you think of anything else, please give me a call," he said, as he and Simmons rose to go. "And thanks for the information."

"Hope it helps, and I hope it leads to something that puts some money in my pocket," Brenda said.

"We'll be sure to let you know," said Simmons, giving her a perfunctory smile as he followed Lucas out the front door.

On the ride back to the police station, Lucas and Simmons discussed what they'd learned from Brenda. The sheet they had run on Higgins showed that, among other things, he had done time for a drunk driving incident several years ago while he was an employee of Wilson Industries. Bill Wilson had been riding with him when they were involved in an automobile accident that had left a woman dead.

"I'd say it's time to pay a visit to Bill Wilson," said Simmons.

"I'd say you're right," replied Lucas.

When they returned to the station, Lucas received a call from a front desk clerk at the Holiday Inn in Baton Rouge. The man said he'd seen Higgins' photo in the newspaper and had recognized him.

"But that wasn't the name he used," explained the desk clerk. "He registered under the name of Warren Edwards. I remember because he stayed at the hotel for several nights and paid his bill in cash."

"Are you sure this is the same man?" Lucas asked.

"Absolutely. There's no doubt in my mind at all."

Lucas thanked the man for calling and said they would get back in touch with him to take his statement.

Monday morning Lucas phoned Bill Wilson at his office.

"Mr. Wilson, this is Lieutenant Lucas. We spoke at your father's funeral." Lucas waited for Bill's grunt of recognition before continuing. "We, that is, my partner and I, would like to come out and talk to you this morning."

"Fine," said Bill, trying to keep the anxiety out of his voice. "I'll make sure I'm available."

After he hung up the phone, Bill nervously pulled out his pack of cigarettes and lit one. Could they have some information on my father, he wondered. Maybe they have something on Higgins. But what? Could they have found Jack's gun? What if Jack hadn't thrown the gun in the water like he was supposed to? Had Jack lied to him? Had he kept the gun to blackmail him? But what good would that do, since the serial numbers had been filed off?

These and other troubling questions raced through Bill's head. Still, by the time Lucas and Simmons entered his office, he appeared calm, composed, and relaxed.

"Lieutenant, I hope your visit means you have something to tell me about my father's case," Bill said, his tone strident.

"Mr. Wilson, we actually have two homicides on our hands. Your father's, of course, and now, a man named Jack Higgins. We're working on both of them right together. Today, we'd like to ask you some questions about Jack Higgins." Lucas took out his notebook. "You're not a suspect, but we're hoping you might be able to fill in some blanks for us."

Bill feigned surprise.

"The Higgins murder? How can I help you there?"

"Did you know Jack Higgins?"

"Sure I did. He used to work for Wilson Industries. In fact, he and I used to frequent the same watering holes before he did time."

"So you knew Jack Higgins had been in prison," Lucas said.

"Lieutenant," Bill said, almost admonishingly, "you know I did. He was driving my car several years ago when he ran off the road and totaled it. A woman who worked at the mill was with us. She was killed. I've never forgiven myself for that." Bill sat down, as if the memory were too heavy to bear. "We were all a little drunk, but Higgins insisted he was fine, so I let him drive."

"Higgins was driving, not you?" Simmons asked.

"Yes. It's all in the police report."

"When was the last time you saw him?" Lucas asked.

"Jack? I met him about a couple of weeks ago at Bubba's Diner," Bill responded. "Lieutenant, why do I get the feeling you're asking questions to which you already know the answers?"

"What was the meeting about?" Lucas asked, ignoring Bill's question.

"He had called me and asked to get together. Told me he was looking for a job. Unfortunately, I had to tell him our company policy does not allow us to hire felons. I offered to loan him some money to help him get back on his feet, but he refused it. Said he'd probably leave town and start somewhere else. I wished him luck."

"When did you hear that he'd been murdered?"

"I read it in the paper."

"Why didn't you contact us with this information?" Simmons asked.

"What information? His death was reported in the paper, for Christ's sake. I figured you knew."

"I'm talking about the fact that you had just gotten together with him a couple of weeks ago."

"Well, I didn't see how it would do anything except make me look bad. I mean, it's not like I knew who killed him. But with my father just murdered, and now Jack Higgins killed—a guy I just recently had a couple of beers with—well, you tell me, Lieutenant, how does that look?"

Lucas, who seemed intent on his notebook, did not answer Bill.

Bill went on sourly, "I'm interested in finding the person who killed my father, which, I'm sorry to say, doesn't appear to be that important to you. If it were, why would you be spending all this time trying to catch whoever put a couple of holes in Jack Higgins?"

Lucas looked up quickly at Bill, his stare intense.

"What makes you think that Jack Higgins was shot twice?" Lucas asked.

Bill's face paled to a chalk color, his mouth as dry as the Sahara Desert. He smiled to compose himself and gave little laugh.

"Just a figure of speech, Lieutenant. I don't know or care how many holes were in his body. In fact, I don't care about Higgins at all. I just want to find out who murdered my father."

"Like I said, Mr. Wilson, we're looking at both murders together." He stood up, and Simmons followed his lead. "We'll be back in touch with you when and if we have something to tell you."

As Lucas and Simmons drove out of the parking lot of Wilson Industries' corporate headquarters, Frank Lucas turned to his partner.

"Jerry, what do you think of Mr. Wilson's answers?"

"They sounded pretty straight," he replied.

"Let me tell you, Jerry, after having spent twenty-five years investigating criminal cases, I have seen many a 'Bill Wilson.' I believe he is my mannn!" Frank said almost singing his last two words. He steered the car down the highway, his mind far from his driving. "Yes, Jerry, he answered straight. But if he had come forward on his own, any information he gave us would have been confidential. So why would he worry about his public image or having others know that he saw Jack prior to his death?"

Simmons considered what Lucas said, but said nothing, thinking. Lucas went on, oblivious to his partner's silence.

"We never released information on how many times Higgins was shot. Now tell me, Jerry, how in the hell did Bill know that?"

"He did look like he had seen a ghost when you asked him how he knew Higgins was shot twice. But then again, maybe he just guessed it."

"Personally, I doubt that," Frank said. "The look on Bill Wilson's face was a look of real worry. I've got a feeling that he's involved in all this, and I'm going to play that card. We don't have enough right now to point a finger, but the pieces are starting to come together. First of all, there's Wilson's involvement with Higgins years ago, in the drunk driving accident. Then Higgins shows up in Plaquemine recently and meets with Bill. Shortly after that meeting, old man Wilson's murdered. And then Higgins is murdered. Maybe it's all coincidence; then again, maybe not." Lucas tapped the steering wheel. "Yessirree, we'll be keeping a close eye on Mr. Bill Wilson."

Lucas spent the remainder of the day doing what he often did when he had an especially tricky case: writing down all the people, events, and clues he had on a large poster board, then sketching out possible links.

Finally, Frank stood up, grabbed his coat, and said, "Jerry it's getting late. Let's call it quits for the day and go get a nice filet mignon with a couple of glasses of beer to celebrate."

"Sounds great," Jerry replied. "But what do we have to celebrate?"

"Jerry," Frank answered, a big grin on his face, "we are celebrating the opening of the door to our investigation."

Early the next morning, as Lucas drove to headquarters, he couldn't get Bill Wilson off his mind. He had spent a sleepless night trying to determine what his next step should be. At the moment he had a lot of coincidence, but little evidence. He decided to focus on tracking down the murder weapon. So far, none had turned up, despite the department's dragging of the fishing lake and an intense search of the wooded area surrounding it.

Lucas ordered several officers to begin canvassing the pawn shops and sporting goods stores in Plaquemine and in nearby towns to find who had purchased a .38 caliber gun over the past six months. When the search in Plaquemine yielded nothing promising, he expanded it to Baton Rouge.

Two days later, Simmons jumped when Lucas slammed down the phone receiver.

"What's up?" he asked.

Lucas ripped a piece of paper off his telephone pad and held it up, a triumphant look on his face.

"Officer Danson just called from outside Baton Rouge. He talked to the owner of a sporting goods store there who sold a nickel-plated .38 caliber Cobra Colt revolver to a Bill Wilson just two months ago." He grabbed his suit coat off the back of his chair. "I'm going down to talk to the guy. You want to come?"

Jerry shook his head. "Can't. I'm waiting for a call on the Berger case. Find me and fill me in when you get back."

It took Lucas less than forty-five minutes to reach Mack's Outdoor Sports located in a strip mall just off Interstate 10 outside Baton Rouge. The owner, Ray Hawkins, identified Bill as the man who had bought the gun. He showed Lucas the application Bill had completed, along with the bill of sale, making copies for him. Driving back to Plaquemine, Lucas had no more doubt. Too many arrows pointed to Bill Wilson. All he had to do was tie them all together.

Later that day, Lieutenant Lucas sat in his office staring at his case board, when Detective Simmons came in.

"What did you find out?" Simmons asked.

"It was Wilson, all right, who bought that weapon. Jerry, he's our guy."

"You're going to have to get around the fact that Bill was in England when his father was murdered," Jerry said

"I don't care if he was in China or on the moon!" Frank bellowed, pounding his fist on the desk. "Bill Wilson comes up everywhere in these two cases. I'm telling you, Jerry, he's in it up to his neck."

"So what's your next move?"

Lucas tapped his pencil on the telephone pad, then grabbed the receiver.

"Let's go pay a call on his wife."

Judy had spent the last few weeks trying to make the best of the difficult situation. Because of unexpected and tragic events in the Wilson family,
she had asked her attorney to put the divorce on hold until he heard from
her. Judy had also told the private investigator, Walter Angelle, to forget trying to document any extramarital affairs in which Bill might be involved until
everything had been settled with the family. Despite her feelings about Bill
and his treatment of her, she did not want to place this additional burden on
the family in their time of grieving.

When Lieutenant Lucas phoned asking to meet with her, she told him
to come right over.

"Good afternoon, Mrs. Wilson," said Lucas when Judy answered the
door. "I appreciate your being able to see us on such short notice." He turned
to Jerry. "This is my partner, Detective Simmons."

Judy pushed the screen door open.

"Please come in," she said graciously.

Sitting on the pristine white sofa, a refreshing tumbler of iced tea on the
glass coffee table in front of him, Lucas began his interview.

"Mrs. Wilson, I've heard that you and your husband are separated. Is
that correct?" Lucas asked.

"Yes, that's right." Judy said. "He moved out of our house several weeks
ago. He lives in one of the guest houses on the grounds."

"Did you know Jack Higgins, the man who was found murdered at the
fishing lake?" Simmons asked.

"No, I didn't. I understand, though, that he worked at Wilson Industries
some time ago. Since our separation, I don't have a lot of close contact with
the family, but I heard through the grapevine at work that he and Bill used to
run around together when Higgins worked at the mill. He's the one who
went to prison after the drunk driving accident." She stopped, her brow fur-
rowed. "I suppose you know about that. That a woman they were with that
night was killed in the accident?"

Lucas nodded. "Mrs. Wilson, have you noticed anything strange about
your husband's behavior lately?"

Judy gave him a steady look.

"First of all, Lieutenant, I don't see much of Bill these days. What I can
tell you, however, is that Bill Wilson today is not the man I fell in love with
and married years ago. His behavior has not been strange 'lately.' His strange

behavior began long ago and has worsened over the years. He would grow violent at times, and I finally became afraid for myself and my son. I've decided to file a divorce, although Bill has promised he will never give me one. And being an almighty Wilson, he thinks no judge around here would ever cross him and grant me a divorce." Judy paused, lifting her iced tea to her lips to take a small sip, then slowly returning the glass to its coaster. "Still, I was ready to start court proceedings. Even after his mother had a stroke I was prepared to go forward. But then, when his father was murdered, I felt the decent thing to do would be to put the divorce on hold, at least until the family had recovered somewhat."

"Do you have any grounds for divorce?"

"I know he's been cheating on me for years. In fact, I hired a private investigator to get the kind of information I would need to document that in court. He put a recording device on the phone here, but Bill rarely uses it since he moved out. He only comes by from time to time to see our son, Mike."

Frank Lucas finished jotting down some notes, then stood up.

"Thank you, Mrs. Wilson. I think that's all for now. We may contact you again later."

"Lieutenant, do you think Bill is somehow involved in the Higgins murder?" asked Judy.

Lucas looked into the wide, startlingly blue eyes, almost losing himself there. He longed to tell Judy what he felt in his gut, but forced himself to be noncommittal.

"We're just trying to follow up any connection at this point," he said. "We'll let you know if anything develops regarding your husband."

On the drive back to the police station, Lucas and Simmons ran into a traffic back up. Parking their car on the shoulder of the road, the two detectives walked up to the front of the snarl, where they saw a truck loaded with watermelons had collided with a passenger car. The truck had spilled most of its load, a sea of pink and green spreading out across the highway. Uniformed officers directed traffic around the mess while a sanitation department crew worked busily to quickly clean it up.

"Jerry, do you know how to tell a good watermelon from a bad one?" Lucas asked, surveying the scene.

"What?" Jerry asked, as though he hadn't quite heard Lucas correctly.

"Do you?"

"Well, " he said, "I know some people thump them and others pull on the stem. Why? You have some surefire way?"

"I sure do. An eighty-year-old watermelon man taught me years ago."

"Really, Frank? You know the secret? Please, please tell me," Jerry implored with mock sincerity.

"Jerry, that old man said, 'Son, the only way you can tell a good watermelon from a bad one is to cut the son of a bitch in two!" He grinned at his partner. "And that's what we are about to do to Bill Wilson."

September 29, 1978

As soon as George Parker boarded his British Airways flight from London to JFK, he sank into his first class seat and closed his eyes. He was exhausted. He'd spent the last several days in negotiations with a legal firm in London noted for their expertise in handling offshore oil drilling leases in the North Sea. George felt their services would mesh well with the work coming his way concerning drilling in the Gulf of Mexico, an industry making a huge impact on Louisiana's economy.

When Parker had received news of Eric Wilson's death, he at first planned to cut his trip short. But David Oliver, the general manager at Wilson Industries, had urged him to stay and complete his work. Parker would miss his long-time friend's funeral but be back to meet with the family for the reading of Eric Wilson's will.

Parker's flight from JFK arrived in Baton Rouge right on time, and his driver delivered him home just before 8 P.M. After fixing himself a gin and tonic, he phoned Kristi Walker and asked her to check with the family as to when they could meet with him to read her father's will. Thirty minutes later, she called back, and the time was set for two days later, Thursday morning at ten-thirty.

Bill, who had to work hard to contain his enthusiasm, arrived a good thirty minutes before the scheduled meeting. Judy, Kristi, and her husband, Steve, and David Oliver arrived just before ten-thirty, as did the representatives of Kellogg and Associates, the Baton Rouge accounting firm handling the bookkeeping for Wilson Industries and the financial services for the family. Lisa Brooks, George Parker's secretary, greeted each visitor, then led them back to the firm's conference room, a well-appointed facility with a massive mahogany table surrounded by plush leather chairs.

"Thank you all for coming," Parker began after everyone was seated. "Let me begin by saying that no one could have been more saddened than I over hearing the news of Eric Wilson's death. He was not only one of the finest people I have ever known, but also like a brother to me. We knew each other from the time we were kids." He paused to collect himself, his distress evident. "My greatest desire is that the Plaquemine police find the person who murdered him and lock that killer away for the rest of his life."

Judy looked over at Bill, who fidgeted with a pencil during Parker's opening remarks. He seems jittery, she thought. As if to give credibility to her thoughts, Bill reached into his jacket pocket and pulled out a pack of cigarettes. Judy watched without any hint of desire to do the same. While she had given up smoking when pregnant, Bill had more than made up for her abstinence by developing a two-pack-a-day habit.

"Sorry, Bill," Parker said, noticing Bill's move. "There's no smoking in our offices. You'll have to wait until we are finished."

With an air of exasperation, Bill Wilson shoved the cigarettes back in his jacket and crossed his legs.

"Sorry," he said, his voice dripping with sarcasm.

"James, do your people have a ledger on the total assets of Wilson Industries?" Parker asked James Kirkpatrick, one of the principals at Kellogg and Associates.

"Yes, we do, George," Kirkpatrick answered. He stood and distributed large manila envelopes to Kristi, Steve, Bill, and Judy. "I have prepared these portfolios for each of the family members with our latest figures on total net worth, assets, liabilities, property owned by the family, and stocks, bonds, and mutual funds. Total net worth is close to two hundred million."

"Thank you, George," Parker said. Then, gesturing to the sealed envelope in front of him, he said, "I have here Eric's last will and testament. If you're all ready…."

Seeing the nods around the table, he opened the sealed envelope then paused to scan the contents.

"Let's see, it begins with several colleges and other educational institutions that Eric and his wife attended to which he wanted to bequeath two hundred and fifty thousand each. He was also a big fan of the work of the American Heart Association, the American Cancer Society, and the Diabetes

Association of America, and has left two hundred and fifty thousand to each of those organizations as well.

"Next, he lists his grandchildren. To Kristi and Steve's children, Jeff and Misty, he has left one million each to be held in a trust until their twenty-first birthdays. To Bill and Judy's son, Michael, he also leaves one million, again to be held in trust until he turns twenty-one. If something should happen to the children and they do not reach their twenty-first birthdays, the money will go to their parents.

"To Judy, Bill's wife, Eric leaves the sum of one million, which she shall receive immediately. To his beloved wife, Debra, Eric has left a trust fund that can be drawn on by Kristi and Bill only for the purpose of paying Debra's medical expenses for as long as she lives.

"Mr. Oliver, Eric has left you the sum of two million dollars and instructed me to emphasize to you that had it not been for your faithful service and business counsel over the years, Wilson Industries would not be where it is today. He asked me to extend his personal thanks to you."

Parker paused here to pour himself a glass of water from one of the pitchers on the table. David Oliver put his head into his hands and his shoulders shook slightly, evidently overwhelmed by his boss's generosity.

Judy noticed Bill tapping his fingers on the table in nervous anticipation. Why is he so edgy, she wondered.

"The remainder of the will," Parker continued, "focuses on the dispensation of the rest of his assets, which leaves the family business to Kristi and Bill." George Parker paused and took off his glasses. Judy couldn't help noticing how old and tired he looked. "I want you to know that your father came to me a couple of weeks before his death asking me to make several changes to his will. We discussed the changes he had in mind, and I made the revisions he requested. This will reflects those changes."

A troubled look clouded Bill's face. The first traces of perspiration appeared on his forehead.

"This may come as a surprise to all of you…but Eric asked me to make Kristi the sole owner of Wilson Industries and of Oakleigh."

A hush fell over the group. Kristi wore a look of utter disbelief. David Oliver stared out the window, and the accounting people began shuffling papers in awkward embarrassment. Finally, Bill broke the silence.

"There's got to be some mistake here," Bill said. "Let me see that document."

"Bill, there's no mistake, and I don't appreciate you questioning my integrity," Parker said. "I am reading from the will."

"And there's nothing about me in there?" Bill asked incredulously.

"You haven't let me finish. You are mentioned here." He looked directly at Bill, his gaze unwavering. "I don't know all the reasons for what your father did. I didn't ask, and he didn't volunteer any information. He has left you the sum of one hundred dollars. I must add, that he originally wanted to leave you nothing, but then decided on the one hundred dollars just to emphasize the fact that he had so little faith in your ability to operate the family business. He also stressed the fact that your behavior over the years and the embarrassment you have caused the family led him to believe that any money left to you would soon be squandered. He felt that Kristi would be much more capable of steering the company in the future. He's allowing you to stay on in your present capacity, and if in Kristi's opinion you turn your life around, you will retain your position and be in line for advancement just like any employee of the company." Parker noted the look of shock on Bill's face, but felt no compassion. "I'm sorry, but that's what he has written."

A painful silence once again fell over the room.

"Well, that's bullshit!" Bill said rising from the table. "Obviously, he was not in his right mind when he approached you about making the changes to the will. I am surprised that you let him go through with this little charade."

"He anticipated a contesting of the will," Parker said, "and had the foresight to have a complete medical and psychiatric evaluation prior to his death. The results, you will find, indicate that he was in total control of his faculties. The medical report is available for you and Kristi to view if you'd like."

"I don't need to see any report," Bill fumed. "I'll see all this straightened out in court."

"Bill," Kristi began, "we don't need to fight this out in court. You know that I'm not going to let you leave with nothing after your years of working in the business. I'll position everything where we…"

Bill turned on her. "Don't patronize me." he sneered. "I don't need a handout. I'm going to see to it that I get what's rightfully mine."

With that Bill stormed out of the room.

"Bill, wait! Bill!" Kristi called after her brother, but he never looked back.

"I guess this meeting is over," Parker said.

Kristi, Steve, Judy, David Oliver, and the accounting people stood and shook hands with George Parker. No one knew quite what to say. George dutifully led them to the elevators and thanked them for coming.

During her drive home, Judy found herself in a state of semi-shock at Eric Wilson's generosity toward her. Thanks to his bequest, she would never have to work again. Of course, the money would not be forthcoming until Bill's contesting of the will had been resolved. Until then, she would continue with her job at Wilson Industries. But she decided she'd contact her attorney and ask the private investigator to resume keeping a watch on Bill's activities.

The following day, Kristi phoned Frank Lucas at the police department and told him that the will had been read.

"How'd it go?" asked Lucas.

"Well, frankly, I was…well, I think we all were shocked. I mean…well, it's best if you talk to George Parker about the specifics. I'm just calling to let you know."

Lucas phoned George Parker and asked if he could come over to talk to him about the will and the murder of Eric Wilson. They made an appointment to meet after lunch in Parker's law offices.

At one-thirty, Lisa ushered Lucas into Parker's office.

"Thanks for meeting with me on such short notice, Mr. Parker," said Lucas, bringing out his notebook and flipping to a blank page. "I'll get right to the point. I'd like to know if there was anything in the will that shocked the family."

"Yes, there was. Eric Wilson left the entire business to his daughter, Kristi."

Lucas let out a soft whistle. "Really? Were there no provisions for his son?"

"None to speak of. Eric never felt that Bill was capable of running Wilson Industries. He didn't want to see the family business evaporate through Bill's recklessness and irresponsibility."

"Had the will always read that way?"

"No. This reflected changes made just a week before Eric was murdered."

"I see. Did Bill or anyone else in the family know about the new will?"

"Not to my knowledge. I suppose Eric could have mentioned it to someone, but I am of the opinion that he did not."

Lucas cocked his head as though he were surprised. "Why do you say that?"

"Because of everyone's evident shock at the terms of the settlement. I'm sure they all thought Eric would have been more, shall we say, concerned about his son."

"And he was not?"

"Lieutenant, Bill had never treated his father with any respect. On the contrary, the more Eric gave to his son, the worse Bill became. I feel that Eric's concern for his son actually prompted his revision of the will. He wanted to ensure that Bill would have to rely on himself and make his way in the world after having coasted for all these years, living on the family name. Bill has cost the family a lot of money. He has worked in the business for years, but it was more or less for show. Bill never made any major decisions or truly felt the need to apply himself to build on what his father and grandfather had established. Kristi was much more concerned about the welfare of Wilson Industries than Bill ever was."

Lucas snapped his notebook closed and rose to leave.

"Thank you for your time, Mr. Parker," Lucas said, extending his hand. "We'll get back to you if we have any more questions."

"Lieutenant, do you have any suspects in the murder?"

"Well, let's just say that pieces are beginning to come together. Not enough right now to make a case against anyone. But we will. It's just a matter of time."

"Can I ask you if Bill is a suspect?" Parker asked suddenly.

"You can ask, but I can't give you an answer right now." He smiled. "Like lawyers, detectives have an obligation to withhold 'privileged' information. The investigation is still ongoing, and anything I said would be speculation." He gave George Parker an appraising look. "Why do you ask? Do you feel that Bill Wilson could have done it?"

The older man shook his head.

"I'm not sure, and like you, I don't want to say anything right now."

Frank Lucas spent the next few days going back over what he had learned and trying to put together the pieces of the puzzle as he saw them. He talked again to Brenda Reed at Bubba's Diner. He drove out to Mack's Sporting Goods and questioned Ray Hawkins again about Bill Wilson's timely purchase of a handgun. He phoned Judy Wilson and went over again Bill's actions during the period of time in which Eric had been murdered and Jack Higgins' body had been found. Still, nothing concrete surfaced.

But he had his gut feelings. After twenty-five years as a cop, he had learned he could trust them as much as anything else. And his gut feeling said Bill Wilson was involved. Too many coincidences, too many connections to Bill Wilson. George Parker had disclosed that Bill stood to lose the most with the new will. Perhaps Bill had planned on there not being enough time for a new will to be drawn up, one in which he would be written out of the picture. Bill had a reputation as a wild and reckless kid and irresponsible rich boy, but had he descended to the point of being able to hire someone to murder his own father?

When Lucas had finally assembled a folder strong enough to present to James McMillan, the Iberville Parish district attorney, he phoned the D.A.'s office for a meeting. During their session, Lucas went over in detail what he had learned from Brenda Reed about Bill's meeting with the Jack Higgins. They also discussed Higgins' connection with Bill years ago, the fatal crash that had sent Higgins to prison and a woman to the morgue. He showed McMillan the copy of the bill of sale for the handgun. They discussed the revised will and how it took Bill Wilson out of the management picture at Wilson Industries.

"All right, Lucas," said McMillan, tossing the last piece of evidence onto the coffee table. "You've done your homework. We'll issue an arrest warrant for Bill Wilson for the murder of Jack Higgins and for hiring the murderer of Eric Wilson."

October 31, 1978

The newspapers, not only in Plaquemine and Baton Rouge but throughout Louisiana, were filled with accounts of the arrest of Bill Wilson on suspicion of murder. The story continued to make the front pages of the tabloids for several days even after Bill had been led away from the guest house at Oakleigh in handcuffs. Bars and boardrooms throughout the state buzzed with rumors, innuendos, and all the latest gossip on what was happening to one of the state's most powerful families.

Bill had been released on two hundred and fifty thousand dollars bail, an amount that sent the district attorney into apoplexy.

"Your Honor!" he cried. "The Wilson family is worth over two hundred million dollars. Let Bill Wilson out on bail, and we'll never see him again."

"I beg to disagree, Your Honor," replied the smooth-as-silk Tony Landero, Bill's high-priced attorney, holding up his hand and ticking off each point on a finger. "First, my client has no serious criminal convictions against him. Second, he is, in fact, a pillar of this community. And, last but not least, he is innocent. He wants very much to have the opportunity to clear his name. He has no intention of fleeing."

The presiding judge, Patricia Stewart, had agreed with Landero and imposed the minimal bail on Bill, which Kristi had promptly posted.

An arraignment date was set for the end of October, on Halloween Day, two weeks after Bill's arrest. The press maintained a constant vigil just off the grounds of Oakleigh, hoping for a word or a photo opportunity. Bill stayed out of public sight, however, leaving his attorney to issue all statements.

Privately, Bill was sweating it out. Lucas's actions had been so fast: the investigation, the questioning, the arrest. What could Lucas know that led him to convince the District Attorney to issue a warrant so quickly? His mind raced back over what had happened with Higgins, trying to remember. Were there any loose ends that he had overlooked? He felt he'd covered himself, but he definitely wasn't sure.

Judy and Kristi were both in shock. Regardless of his track record as a reckless rounder and a worthless husband, neither of them could imagine Bill having anything to do with Higgins' murder, much less the death of Bill's own father. Kristi had been especially supportive of Bill, immediately posting bail for her brother. Bill accepted her offers of help, but with a cool reserve. He could handle this, he assured her. "Concentrate on running Wilson Industries," he told her. "We'll sort out our differences about ownership of the company when the smoke clears."

If Bill had been concerned during the arrest, he became noticeably troubled during the arraignment phase of the proceedings. After both sides had presented their cases for and against charging Bill Wilson with the murder of Jack Higgins, Judge Stewart deliberated for only two hours before ordering Bill Wilson bound over to a grand jury on the charge of first degree murder. The trial was set for the first week of December.

Bill, still free on bail, had become a nervous wreck. He retreated into his home, didn't go to work, and seldom saw or talked to Kristi, her husband, anyone. He no longer visited his comatose mother in the hospital. He did still make his weekly visit to see Mike, as he didn't have to leave the grounds to do so. On each visit, Judy refused to allow Bill to take Mike anywhere and was present during most of the time he spent with their son.

The one person Bill did spend time meeting with was his attorney, Tony Landero. George Parker had been the family attorney, often called on during Bill's years as a wild and reckless youth. Whenever he needed an occasional reprieve on some minor infraction or misdemeanor, George had come to the rescue. But this was a first-degree murder charge. Parker specialized in corporate law and handling the legal affairs of heavy hitters like Eric Wilson. He was not the man that Bill wanted in his corner in a murder trial, when his life was on the line. Nor could he be sure Parker, such a long-time and close friend of his father, would even take his side in this murder case. No, he wanted a pro who had no doubt he could win Bill's case.

Tony Landero had earned his reputation as a tough trial attorney, having won several high-profile cases for Baton Rouge and New Orleans underworld figures. He had also successfully pled down charges on countless other cases many of his colleagues wouldn't even touch. Looking to further boost his name, Landero eagerly accepted the challenge of defending one of the state's most recognizable names in a shocking murder trial, especially when he examined the evidence and could see it was mostly circumstantial. Nothing actually connected his client to the murder of Jack Higgins. A murder weapon had never been found, and the fact that Bill had purchased a handgun shortly before his father had been murdered was hardly an indictment of Bill as Jack Higgins' killer. After each meeting with Landero, Bill's spirits lifted, and a bit of his old confidence returned as he realized the state's case was purely speculative.

The first day of the trial in Judge Stewart's courtroom opened to a standing-room-only crowd. In addition to the legions of media present, Judy, Kristi, and Steve sat in the audience, along with George Parker and an assortment of interested employees from Wilson Industries.

The first two weeks of the trial went just as Landero had predicted. All the evidence that district attorney McMillan and his leading prosecutor, Larry Bishop, presented was suggestive, but the state had been unable to tie that evidence conclusively to Bill Wilson.

Yes, Bill had purchased a .38 caliber handgun, but Jack Higgins was killed with a 9mm weapon. A killer using a .38 had murdered Bill's father. Landero reminded the jury that they were trying Bill Wilson for Higgins' murder. No connection had been established between the two. More important, no murder weapon in the Higgins case had yet been found.

Yes, Bill had met with Jack Higgins prior to his death, but as a former employee of Wilson Industries, it was logical that an ex-convict would approach his former friend and employer for a job. The prosecution had established no other ties between Bill and Higgins during that period of time.

Yes, Bill had been written out of his father's will. But what had that to do with the murder of Higgins? Wasn't Higgins just an acquaintance of Bill's whom the prosecutor could not link as a hired murderer by Bill? The jury was reminded constantly there was no connection between Bill and his father's murder. The only issue before them was whether the state could prove beyond the shadow of a doubt, that Bill Wilson murdered Jack Higgins. They were to consider only the evidence in this case. The first few rounds of the fight went to the defense. Frank Lucas watched and worried, afraid his case was slipping away from him.

On the tenth day of the trial, as Judge Stewart announced a recess for lunch, Lucas remained in his seat, deep in thought. He could see the prosecution's case against Bill might not be strong enough to convince a jury. What else could he do, what other information could he dig up that would undeniably tie Bill to Higgins' murder?

As the spectators in the courtroom rose and shuffled out the back doors, Lucas idly watched a reporter as he closed his notebook and turned off a small tape recorder he had placed on the floor next to him.

A light went on in Lucas's brain.

He remembered Judy Wilson mentioning a private investigator she had retained had installed a recording device on their phone after she and Bill had separated. Although she had said Bill seldom took phone calls there, there was still a chance that someone had phoned him and he could have spoken to them without Judy's knowledge. It was worth a try.

Lucas met Judy in the hallway after the courtroom had cleared for the luncheon recess.

"Mrs. Wilson, you told me once that you had a recording device installed on your phone."

"Yes, Lieutenant, that's true."

"I'd very much like to listen to the tape recordings of the conversations on that device if you don't mind."

"Not at all," Judy said. "I can't imagine that there's anything on them that might help you, though. Like I said, Bill didn't take many calls there after we separated and he moved into the guest house. I haven't even listened to any of the tapes. The divorce proceedings were pretty much put on hold with Mr. Wilson's death and then Bill's arrest. But you're welcome to the tapes to see if there is something there."

"I'd like to get them right away."

"Fine. We can go to my house right now."

Lucas followed Judy Wilson in his own car. Once home, she told the lieutenant to have a seat, while she went up to the attic where the recorder had been installed. In a few minutes, Judy returned with a sack of small audiotapes.

"Hope these help you," she said as she handed the bag to Lucas. Then she smiled and added, "As long as you're going through them, will you let me know if you hear anything that might help me in the divorce?"

Lucas nodded. "It's the least I can do."

Lucas didn't return to the courtroom that afternoon, but turned his total attention to the audiotapes. Most of the afternoon passed without the tapes yielding anything more interesting than Judy's routine conversations. Then, suddenly, he knew he had found what he'd been looking for. A male caller had phoned, asking for Bill. When Bill answered the phone, Higgins anxiously spat out who he was. On hearing Higgins' voice, Bill had become agitated. Higgins told Bill he was tired of waiting and wanted to get the job done. Bill had cut Higgins off and arranged to meet him that evening at the lake outside town.

Bingo, thought Lucas. Higgins had identified himself, and Lucas could tie Bill Wilson to a meeting at the spot where Higgins had been murdered. Here was something concrete the district attorney could confront Bill with and then watch Bill squirm as he tried to explain it. Lucas surmised that Bill had probably arranged to meet Higgins at the lake on more than one occasion, and on their last meeting, Bill had murdered him. Whether he had killed Higgins to eliminate any witnesses to their contract for the murder of his father would be immaterial.

It was almost four-thirty in the afternoon when he had finished listening to all the tapes. Court had adjourned for the day, and Lucas went straight to the district attorney's office to present what he had found to McMillan and his people.

They were huddled around a conference table in McMillan's office when Lucas walked in without knocking.

"Kind of sudden isn't it, Lieutenant?" McMillan asked.

"When you hear what I want to play for you, you'll see why I'm in a hurry," Lucas said.

He plugged in the recorder and turned on the tape. He explained to McMillan and Bishop that it had been installed in Bill Wilson's home when he and his wife separated. Judy had hoped to find some proof of Bill's philandering, but the tapes ended up revealing much more.

When Lucas played the conversation between Bill and Higgins, McMillan and Bishop lit up. Taped conversations, especially when the people being taped were not aware that their conversations were being recorded, would not be admissible as evidence in a court of law, but they definitely tied Bill to Higgins' murder. Realizing that his role in killing Higgins was known, even if the police could not act on it, what would Bill do? Could the district attorney then implicate Bill in his father's murder, for which he could then be charged? Would all this be enough to sweat Bill into copping a plea to try to avoid the death penalty? McMillan felt it was worth asking the judge for a continuance on the grounds of needing to examine newly found evidence. That might make Bill sweat a little more, and Lucas knew that nervous people made mistakes. It was worth a try.

The next morning, when court convened at ten, McMillan asked if he and the defense could approach the bench. Judge Stewart allowed them to come forward.

"Your honor," McMillan began, "the state would like to request a recess in order to present new evidence to the defense that we feel has a direct bearing on this case."

"Your honor, we object," Landero said surprised. "We've heard nothing about any new evidence."

"That's exactly why we want to present this, your honor. We just came into possession of evidence that we feel the defense and Mr. Wilson will want to hear."

"Your honor, we see no need to postpone the closing arguments that were to begin today. The prosecution obviously realizes that it has no case and is stalling for time to try another door. The court understands…."

"The court is well aware of what it understands, Mr. Landero," Judge Stewart said. "Mr. McMillan, is this new evidence ready to be presented to the defense attorneys and then admitted as evidence?"

"It is, your honor."

"In that case, I see no reason why a postponement until this afternoon would jeopardize the proceedings. I will postpone proceedings until three this afternoon. Will that give you time to go over the evidence with defense counsel, Mr. McMillan?"

"It will, your honor."

"In that case, court is recessed until three this afternoon."

Landero walked with McMillan to his desk.

"So what is this new evidence we need to look at?" he asked.

"Let's get to my office," McMillan said, gathering his documents and placing them in his briefcase.

Bill Wilson looked confused.

"What's going on?" he asked Landero when the attorney returned to his desk.

"They want us to look at some new evidence they are going to present," Landero said. "Bill, I hope we're not in for any surprises here. Is there anything you need to tell me about what they might have?"

The beads of perspiration again returned to Bill's forehead.

"I, uh, I can't think of anything they could have," he stammered.

McMillan and Larry Bishop led Tony Landero and Bill Wilson down the hall and up one flight of stairs to McMillan's office on the third floor of the Plaquemine Parish Court House. When they entered the district attorney's office, a secretary was seated in front of a table that held a transcription machine.

"Well, where is this new evidence you supposedly have just uncovered?" Landero asked.

"Mr. Landero, we have just learned of the existence of a tape recording of a phone conversation that links Mr. Wilson to the murder of Jack Higgins," McMillan said.

"That's bullshit!" Bill thundered.

"Calm down, Bill," Landero said. "James, you know as well as I do that even if such a tape exists, it can't be admitted as evidence in a situation like this. Where did this mystery tape come from?"

"We're not at liberty to say right now," McMillan answered, "but I assure you it's authentic, even if we can't present it in court."

"You can't even mention it," Landero added. "If this is all you've got, then this meeting is over. We don't need to…."

"Where did this tape come from?" Bill asked. "Is this something that my wife supposedly came up with? I haven't even lived at home for the past few months. She couldn't have…."

"Bill, don't say anything else," Landero cautioned his client. "Gentlemen, I'm going to consult with my client in my office. We'll see you at three this afternoon when court reconvenes, and if there's nothing else, we'll be ready to begin closing arguments. And, I might add, we expect that the judge will have some strong words for you on requesting a postponement on evidence that you knew was inadmissible. Good morning, gentlemen."

Tony Landero and Bill Wilson rose and walked out of McMillan's office. McMillan motioned to the transcriber to leave as well.

"It was a gamble, but it looks like it failed," Bishop said. "I don't think Wilson is spooked enough over what could be on a tape that he knows can't be used against him."

"Maybe," Lucas said. "But I've got a hunch that Bill Wilson will want to know exactly what we have and how it could or couldn't hurt him. I think it's worth keeping an eye on him this afternoon to see what he's up to."

"Might be a good idea," McMillan said. "But Landero's right. We really don't have much else. If we could get him and Wilson to listen to the tape, we might have a better shot, but there's no way we can force that. Landero knows that, and Bill stands to gain nothing by sitting at a playing of the tape. I guess we'll have to go with what we've got and present closing this afternoon."

"I still want to keep an eye on Wilson for a while," Lucas said. "If he's even a little bit nervous, it might cause him to be careless. I want to be there if he does."

"Well, I guess there's nothing we can do here," McMillan said. "We'll see you when we reconvene."

December 15, 1978

Bill left his attorney at the entrance to the courthouse, agreeing to meet him at two-thirty in the courtroom to be ready for the closing arguments.

As he walked down the street, Bill was oblivious to everyone or everything around him. His mind raced back to the night at the lake, back to his meeting with Higgins at the diner, back to his father's funeral. So many details! If he had overlooked something, it could be his undoing. But what? Why would McMillan and Lucas appear so eager to present a tape unless it held a conversation between Bill and Higgins that could tie Bill to the murder? Where had he been each time he had spoken with Higgins? He'd made several calls from public telephones, but no one could have traced those calls. Where else?

His aimless wandering led him to a bar that was just opening. He decided to go in for a drink.

"Dewar's on the rocks," he told the bartender.

Bill downed his drink, hoping the alcohol would clear his head. Where could he have been recorded when speaking to Higgins?

And then it hit him. That afternoon at Judy's, he thought, when Higgins had called him. That's the only place it could have been. Every other conversation Bill had initiated, always from a different phone booth. But why would Judy be taping phone calls at their house?

The pieces suddenly fit together. The divorce. Judy must have had her phone bugged, hoping to get something on him.

Bill slammed his fist down on the bar, causing the bartender to throw a dark look in his direction. Shit, Bill thought, she'd gotten something all right. He'd better pay Judy a visit.

Bill threw a few bills on the counter and hurried out the door. Once on the street he sprinted to his car and drove as fast as the law allowed to Oakleigh.

As he pulled up, he saw Judy and Mike climbing out of her car, each carrying a sack of groceries. The Mercedes skidded to a stop, and Bill jumped out.

Judy looked up, startled. "Bill, what are you doing here?"

"Came to see you," he said coldly. "Hi there, big boy," he said to his son.

Mike looked at his father, but didn't answer.

Judy turned the key in the door and pushed it open. "Well, come on in," she said. "Mike, you can just put the groceries in the kitchen and then go on outside and play."

"Okay, Mom," he said.

Judy walked into the kitchen and placed her sack of groceries on the counter. When she turned around, she found Bill standing directly in front of her. A feeling of dread came over her.

"Is there anything you want to tell me?" he asked, a look of thunder in his eyes.

"What are you talking about?" Judy asked.

Bill slapped her across the face.

"Don't play cute with me, Judy," he seethed.

"I told you once I'd never let you hit me again," Judy said, looking right into his eyes. "Now, get out of here before I—"

Bill slapped her again, harder. Blood trickled from the side of Judy's mouth. Then a white-hot fury overtook her, and she raised her fist, ready to fight back. But Bill was stronger and quicker. He grabbed her arms and squeezed them behind her. The pain took her breath away.

"Do you have any tapes or other electronic bullshit around here?" he asked.

Judy ignored his question. "This is going to look great in the divorce," she cried. "Go ahead. Slap me again. Let's see how tough you are. Let's see how these bruises and blood are going to look when I show them to the judge."

"You're not going to have a chance to show them to any judge," Bill spat. "Now I'm going to ask you again. Do you have any little devices around here that I need to know about?"

"There's nothing here," Judy cried, the pain in her arms and shoulders becoming unbearable.

"Wrong answer, Judy. Try again!" He squeezed her arms even tighter.

"The police took them!" she screamed. "There's nothing here!"

"What did they take?" Bill said.

"Tapes! Audio tapes!"

"Tapes of what?" yelled Bill, his grip tightening.

Judy squirmed in pain. "You're hurting me, you bastard! Let go and I'll tell you!" Reluctantly, Bill let his hands drop. Judy immediately turned away from him and began rubbing her arms and shoulders. After a moment, she said, "I had a machine installed to tape phone conversations. I knew you were running around, and I hired a private investigator to get information on your activities. I needed it…needed to have evidence for the divorce."

Bill stared at her, his anger rising up within him, the blood rushing to his head, the sweat dripping down his face. So the police did have a tape of his conversation with Higgins. He saw his entire scheme collapsing. A great force of raging fury engulfed him. Quickly, violently, he spun Judy around. He wrapped his hands around her throat, watching with cold cruelty as her eyes grew wide in horror. From her gaping mouth came a horrible rattle. Bill tightened his grip.

"I should have had Higgins kill you, too!" he screamed.

"Dad, don't do that! You're hurting Mommy!" Mike stood in the doorway to the kitchen, his eyes wild with fear.

Bill didn't respond, his eyes fixed on Judy's contorted face as it turned a sickly purple. Her body slowly went limp like a rag doll.

Mike rushed to his father and desperately tried to pull him away from his mother.

Without looking at the child, Bill removed one hand from Judy's throat and slapped Mike, slamming the boy back against the kitchen counter. Mike looked around the room, the urgency to save his mother overcoming his fear. His eyes stopped on the drawer next to the stove, remembering the knives he was never supposed to touch. He raced across the room, opened the drawer, quickly grabbed the largest knife he could find, and ran to his father, plunging the knife into his back with all his might.

Bill screamed in pain. He dropped Judy and flailed at the blade stuck in his lower back, pulling it out with a grunt. Then he turned on Mike, his eyes burning with a fiery rage. The knife still in his hand, he advanced on his son.

"Freeze!" a voice yelled. "Drop the knife! Now!"

Bill looked up to see Lieutenant Lucas crouching in the doorway leading to the dining room, his .38 revolver pointed, drawing a bead on Bill's head. He looked down at the knife in his hands, seeming almost bewildered at finding it there. He dropped it and stepped back.

"On the floor, face down, hands behind your head! Now!" Lucas yelled.

Bill dropped to his knees and placed his hands in front of him as he lowered himself to the ground. Then he placed his hands behind his head, his fingers interlaced.

Lucas ran to where Judy was lying still clutching her throat.

"Are you okay?" he asked.

She nodded, though she said nothing. Mike ran to his mother's side, tears streaming down his face.

"She's going to be all right, son," Lucas said.

With his revolver still trained on Bill, Lucas picked up the kitchen phone and called for a squad car and an ambulance. Then he slapped his handcuffs on Bill Wilson's wrists and jerked him upright. Bill winced, but said nothing, his head down and eyes still glazed.

The squad car and the ambulance arrived simultaneously. The paramedics examined Judy and insisted she let them take her to the emergency room, where a doctor could examine her for possible damage to her trachea. She looked hesitantly at Mike.

One of the paramedics squatted down to be at eye level with the boy.

"How would you like to ride in an ambulance?" he asked. When Mike looked uncertain, he added, "Hey, we'll even put the siren on. All the cars will have to get out of our way."

Mike brightened a bit. "Okay," he answered, his hand firmly holding his mother's.

Lieutenant Lucas loaded Bill Wilson, still in cuffs, into the squad car.

Bill gazed out the window in a state of semi-consciousness. The familiar sights of Oakleigh, of Wilson Industries, of Plaquemine—these would all become just a memory to him where he was going. Life as he had known it was over.

With Bill in jail, Lucas quickly obtained a search warrant for the guest house, and he and Simmons set about making a thorough search. Hidden in the back of one of the kitchen cupboards they discovered the black satchel. Bill had evidently hid it away, thinking he would have time to get rid of its contents. Inside the satchel, they found Higgins' wallet, car keys, and the

receipt from the hotel in Baton Rouge, along with legal papers, jewelry, and a
.32 caliber Taurus handgun, all presumably from Eric Wilson's safe.

The following day, Lucas met with Bill and his lawyer at the Plaquemine
County Jail where he was being held.

"Mr. Wilson, looks like you'll be charged not only with Higgins' murder, but also with hiring him to kill your father. You see, we found the black
satchel, Mr. Wilson." He paused, watching Bill take in the meaning of his
words. Slowly, the defiance ebbed out of Bill Wilson's eyes. "Things will go a
lot easier on you if you decide to cooperate with us."

Tony Landero leaned over and whispered into his client's ear.

"Give us a few moments, won't you?" the lawyer asked Lucas.

Ten minutes later, when Lucas returned to the interrogation room, Bill
was ready to talk. He confessed to hiring Jack Higgins to murder his father,
then killing Higgins to keep him silent. In exchange for the information,
Lieutenant Lucas promised not to ask for the death penalty.

A week later, when court had reconvened, the Honorable Judge Stewart
addressed the jury. "Have all the members of the jury come to a conclusion
as to sentencing?"

"We have, Your Honor." The foreman passed a paper to the bailiff. He
handed it to Judge Stewart who read it to herself, then handed it back to the
bailiff to give to the foreman.

"Will the defendant please rise."

Bill rose, his face blank, devoid of any emotion.

"Please read the sentence," instructed the judge.

"We, the jury, sentence the defendant, Bill Wilson, to life in prison without the possibility of parole."

The Honorable Judge Stewart addressed Bill, who stood unremorseful
as she spoke.

"Bill Wilson, the jury has justly punished you, as you have confessed to
the murder of Jack Higgins and hiring him to kill your father, Eric Wilson. I
must say, Mr. Wilson, in the twenty-four years I have sat on this bench, I have
never come across a case quite such as yours, and I hope I never live to see
another one like it."

With that Bill Wilson was handcuffed and taken away. The news media
raced to file their stories.

June 4, 2002

"Dad, are you listening to me? Dad, Dad!"

Mike Wilson's thoughts abruptly snapped back from the past to the present.

"What, Peter?" he asked, a bit dazed.

"Dad, haven't you been listening to what I have been telling you?" Peter looked at him with the sincere concern of an eight-year-old. "What's the matter, Dad? You've been acting kind of strange all afternoon."

"Sorry, son. I...well, I got a phone call earlier, and it's been on my mind."

Mike smiled reassuringly at his son, but inwardly he felt exhausted and emotionally drained. Ever since the warden had called that morning, his mind had been inadvertently sliding back into the past, remembering his own childhood and the man who had made it a nightmare.

"Tell me, did you enjoy your party?" Mike asked, rumpling Peter's short, auburn hair.

"Yeah! It was great!" Peter said. "It was so much fun having all my friends come over. And did you see all the presents I got?"

"I did. So many, I think we're going to have to take some back."

"No way!" cried Peter, then seeing the grin on his dad's face, he punched him in the arm. "Come on, let's play catch. I want to try out my new glove."

"After dinner. Why don't you go and play with some of the other gifts your friends gave you until we're ready to eat."

Mike followed Peter out of the office and went downstairs into the kitchen where his wife, Rebecca, and mother, Judy, were preparing dinner.

"Hello, you beautiful young ladies!" he exclaimed.

His mother laughed.

"I wish!" she said, as she stirred the gravy on the stove.

Mike gave her a hug. "You'll always look good to me, Mom."

Rebecca put her arms around Mike and gave him a squeeze. "You came just at the right time, honey. Dinner is almost ready."

Rebecca called Peter, and the four sat down, chatting happily over Peter's favorite dinner of roast beef, mashed potatoes, green beans, and lots of gravy. After they finished dinner and Peter had left the table, Mike told the two women about the unexpected phone call he had received from the warden.

"He said Dad is dying and he wants to see me before he…goes," Mike confided.

Rebecca took his hand. "I thought you seemed preoccupied today. No wonder."

Judy gave him a sympathetic look. "I know it's a tough decision, Mike. Give it some careful thought. I wouldn't blame you at all for not going to see him. No child should have to go through what he put you through. And, after all, it's almost as though he died years ago."

That night as Mike got into bed, his thoughts were on all those who directly or indirectly had been involved in his father's case. Brenda Reed had purchased a fish house restaurant with the reward money she'd received and had made a good living for herself. Lieutenant Lucas had retired over ten years ago and moved to Jacksonville, Florida, where he spent his days fishing. Detective Simmons had been promoted to captain and was in charge of criminal investigations. Tony Landero, his father's defense attorney, and Larry Bishop, the prosecuting attorney were both still practicing law. James McMillan had gone into politics and was serving his district as a U.S. congressman. The judge, Mrs. Patricia Stewart, had left the bench and moved to upstate New York. Mr. Oliver, the former general manager of the Wilson Company, had passed away, three days short of his seventy-third birthday. His Aunt Kristi had sold the Wilson Company, and the whole family had moved to Beverly Hills. Mike's grandmother, Debra, had never regained consciousness and had died five months after the trial. His mother, Judy, had married a very successful lawyer and lived just five miles away.

Mike thought of his life, too. He had finished high school in Plaquemine and gone on to college at Louisiana State University in Baton Rouge. He had later earned his law degree and gone into criminal law. In his senior year at LSU he had met Rebecca, who was studying to become a special ed teacher, and they had married soon after. While he tried to live in the present, where his life was happy and fulfilled, the dark events and experiences of the past were always there, somehow shadowing his future.

After spending a sleepless night, he came to a decision: He would go to see his father.

As he drove to the prison hospital, Mike Wilson's thoughts again returned to the house where more than twenty years ago he had gone to the aid of his mother. The visions of that day—the desperate fear in his mother's eyes, the knife in his hands, the uncontrollable rage on his father's face, the blade of the knife disappearing into his father's back, the police lieutenant holding the gun on his father—were as vivid to him as if they had taken place that very morning. No amount of time could erase the intensity of the emotions he had felt, the scars that had been inflicted that day, not just to him but to his mother, Aunt Kristi, and the rest of the family.

Although Mike had not been allowed to go to his father's trial, he had later read about them, the gaps filled in little by little by his mom and aunt. He did remember one quote he had read in an old newspaper clipping, made by the judge. When she had pronounced sentence on his father, she had stressed that in over twenty years on the bench, she had never witnessed such cold, ruthless, calculated acts of viciousness.

A cold, calculating, vicious killer. This was who Mike's dad was.

When Mike arrived at the Louisiana State Correctional Facility, he sat in his car outside the gate for some time, still questioning his decision. If only *I* could get a reprieve from the governor, he laughed to himself. Since none came, he sighed and drove to the gate where he showed his identification to the officer on duty. Following the officer's directions, he parked in the area for the after-hours visitors' entrance used for emergencies. Once again, a guard checked his i.d. and then verified Mike's story with the warden's office. Finally, Mike was issued a visitor's pass and led to the prison hospital, a dark, dreary facility with the unmistakable feel of death.

Bill Wilson's bed was the third from the door in a Spartan ward of ten beds. What a far cry this was from the top-shelf luxury that Bill had lived in most of his life, Mike thought

Seeing the pitiful figure lying there, the bitterness Mike had always felt for his father evaporated. Though only sixty-five, Bill was a shriveled, dying shell of a man. His hair was completely gone from the chemotherapy and radiation treatments he had undergone. His eyes were sunken into his head, and his skin was drawn so tautly against his cheekbones that he already had the appearance of a living skull. His grey color reminded Mike of a corpse. He looked to be a living skeleton with skin and bones.

As Mike approached Bill's bed, the older man abruptly opened his eyes. Recognition sparked in the eyes, and with his left index finger he motioned to Mike to bend down close to his face. When Mike did so, his father touched his hand and whispered in his ear.

"Mike, my son, is it too late to tell you I'm sorry for all the things that I have done?"

Bill Wilson turned his head and coughed, a punishing hacking cough that frightened Mike. He noticed that there was blood on the handkerchief that his father held clutched in his shriveled hand.

Mike looked at his father, surprised that he felt no anger, no lingering hatred, only empathy for the feeble, old man dying in the bed. Bill Wilson had fallen as far as anyone could fall, having lost his family, his empire, his future, and now, his final battle against death. Mike realized there was no sense in feeling anything but pity for his father.

Mike reached out and touched his father's hand. Bill looked up at him once more and then closed his eyes. Mike stood there for a few minutes staring down at his father. As he turned to leave the room, Mike had tears in his eyes and a lump in his throat. He whispered to himself, "I'm sorry too, Dad, for what I did to you."

Mike slowly walked away from his father's bed. As he did so, a guard joined him and walked with him out of the hospital ward. Turning in his visitor's badge, Mike was escorted to the exit by another somber-faced employee.

Outside, the slight breeze brought welcome relief from the fetid air in the hospital. During his ride home, Mike knew that the haunting, dark cloud that had hung over him all these years was gone. The *Vicious Mind* of Bill Wilson had been put to rest. Mike was now finally able to close the door on his past and open the door to his future and the new life he would live.

About the AUTHOR

Born January 30, 1932 on the Greek island of Evia, Plato Papajohn is a survivor of World War II and the Greek Civil War. Finally immigrating to the United States as a young sixteen-year old boy, he became a naturalized citizen in a year's time and was later drafted in the U. S. Army during the Korean Conflict. His early experiences during wartime are the topic of his well-received, first book, *Stairway to Heaven* (available on Ebay).

A successful entrepreneur and avid reader, Papajohn's lifelong dream was to become an author. After raising four children and securing the future of his family business, Papajohn is now making his dream a reality. *Vicious Mind* is his first murder mystery. Currently, he is editing his second mystery novel, *The Avenger*.

Papajohn and his wife reside in Birmingham, Alabama.

Stairway to Heaven
By Plato Papajohn

This is the story of an amazing true-life adventure. It all starts just before World War II, on the Greek island of Evia. Where an eleven-year-old boy named Plato, suddenly has the beauty of his beloved island and majestic mountains fall into the hands of the Nazis. This idyllic world will soon turn into a nightmare, as his life suddenly becomes a struggle to survive. A young innocent child is transformed into a cold, unfeeling creature that will be willing to do whatever is necessary to keep him and his family alive for the next few horrifying years. For those people who have never felt the cold breath of war, or death and starvation, they cannot relate to the haunted dreams of those who have.

This book will show you many experiences of brutality, intrigue, betrayal, cunning, and revenge. Plato who has always been a survivor, had been greatly hardened by the experience of the Nazi occupation of his island and the civil war. Now the young boy from the tiny village of Evia must travel to a new life here in the United States of America, where he must face many new challenges as he becomes familiar with his new homeland. This is a place where he questions the purpose of his existence. In where he must rediscover his relationship with God, who he thought had long abandoned him. This journey will take you not only spiritually, but also worldly through the life of an extraordinary human being, as he becomes a husband, a father, and a very successful businessman. In his new life, in the New World Plato is able to find the true gift that fills him with happiness, joy, and love. This book is a powerful rendering of an extraordinary mans existence. *Stairway to Heaven* will undoubtedly capture your heart.